Northern Woods

Northern Woods

Amy Hepp

FIFTH
AVENUE
PRESS

Northern Woods

Fifth Avenue Press is a locally focused and publicly owned publishing imprint of the Ann Arbor District Library. It is dedicated to supporting the local writing community by promoting the production of original fiction, nonfiction, and poetry written for children, teens, and adults.

Printed in the United States of America

First Printing 2022

Layout and Illustration: Ann Arbor District Library

Editor: Amy Sumerton

ISBN: 978-1-956697-09-4 (Paperback); 978-1-956697-10-0 (Ebook)

Fifth Avenue Press

343 S Fifth Ave

Ann Arbor, MI 48104

fifthavenue.press

For my Dad, who loved the Boundary Waters.

Chapter One

EMMA LOADED her students onto the bus and gathered her lesson plans. The early dismissal allowed her to beat the rush-hour traffic out of Chicago. She picked up Chinese takeout for dinner and navigated the wet neighborhood streets as trick-or-treaters scampered from house to house.

The landscapers had neglected to rake the leaves in front of the suburban home she'd shared with Craig for the last seven years, and she made a mental note to call the company tomorrow. She pushed open the front door with her hip and tossed her teacher bag and purse in the foyer. Their formal living room led to the kitchen, and she deposited the food on the granite island. The shower ran upstairs. She lifted one eyebrow and bit her lower lip. Craig was home early today. Their schedules were out of sync and their love life needed a spark. A spontaneous, sexy shower might be the answer. She entered their bedroom suite, kicked off her shoes, and said, "Hi, honey, I picked up Chinese food for—"

She entered the bathroom, pushing a pile of clothes with the door. A black thong was draped over the mirror and a paisley tie lay in the sink. Noise in the shower captured her attention, and she looked over to see Craig's firm backside clenched as he thrusted into his young, blond assistant, currently splayed against the marble shower wall. Craig's hips gyrated to a beat, and he moaned, "Baby, baby." His assistant gasped and pointed at Emma. "Baby, what's wrong? Come on, move with me," Craig said in his deep voice. His assistant shook her head and covered her breasts with her hands.

Craig turned around and gasped. "Why are you home?"

"Early dismissal. Halloween." Emma spun on her heel and tore out of the bathroom. She picked up her shoes and ran downstairs.

Craig scrambled out of the shower and whipped a towel around his waist. He chased her down the stairs. Water streamed down his muscular legs and pooled around his bare feet. His flawless face glistened with water and his six-pack abs moved with heavy breaths. Emma flung her teacher bag and purse over her shoulder. Craig grasped her elbow. "Wait. Let's talk."

Emma stepped back from the puddled water on the hardwood floor and yanked the door open. "We're done."

Sun hit the crystal vase on the table beside her bed and a rainbow of color splashed onto the wall of her parents' guestroom. Her mom couldn't wait to remodel her bedroom and transform it into a guest room when she'd left for college twelve years ago. A mahogany sleigh bed with a lush white duvet replaced her tiny twin. A neutral gray wall color and a framed piece of modern art replaced Emma's beloved pink walls and movie posters. Her cross-country trophies and violin were tucked away in the closet along with the rest of her childhood memories. She hugged the tear-soaked pillow and rubbed her head while she called in sick to school and sent her team-mates an email.

The image of her husband as he made love to another woman in their shower ran through her mind on a continuous loop, so she heaved herself out of bed and stood in front of the mirror. Tangled, wavy brown hair and red rimmed eyes stared back at her. She dug an old pair of leggings and a University of Illinois sweatshirt from a bin in her closet and pulled them on over her small frame. After a trip to the bath-room, she stumbled downstairs. Her retired parents read the *Chicago Tribune* and drank coffee in the sunny, yellow kitchen.

"Good morning, dear. How did you sleep?" asked her mother as she read the morning news. Her mom, dressed for the day in wool slacks and a sweater, dined at the breakfast table in perfect hair and makeup while Emma shook her head and swiped tears from her gritty eyes.

"I'm sure Craig can provide you with an explanation for his indiscretion. Why don't you call him after you fix your hair and repair your splotchy face," said her mother.

Emma poured herself a cup of tea and leaned against the counter. "I need a divorce lawyer."

Her dad, still in his robe, peered at Emma from behind his paper.

Her mother folded her section of the paper into a neat square, pumped her crossed leg, and regarded Emma. "Don't be silly. You can't get a divorce over one tiny lapse in judgment. Craig is wonderful. I'm sure it was a misunderstanding."

Emma slid a piece of bread into the toaster and slammed down the lever. "Craig cheated on me—I need a divorce and an apartment."

Her mother removed her glasses and raised her voice. "But you can't leave him yet; I don't have a grandchild. And what about the club? Craig's family vouched for our membership in the club. If you divorce him, what will happen?"

Emma gripped her hot tea mug and said, "He cheated. I'm leaving him."

"I wonder what drove him into the arms of another woman," her mom mused.

Emma furrowed her brow and glared at her.

Her mom pursed her lips and picked up her paper again. "Well, I think you're making an enormous mistake."

Emma sipped her tea. "You usually do."

Emma retreated upstairs to her former bedroom with her tea and toast and stewed over her mother's comment. Did she drive Craig to cheat when she pestered him for a baby? She nagged him about his piles of crap and clothes strewn about the house and it irritated him, but she liked a tidy home. She picked a loose thread on the duvet and twisted it around her finger. Did her relentless school schedule drive him away? She wiped away her tears and shook her head. Regardless of whatever problems festered in their marriage, he broke their vows. He cheated, and she needed an apartment. A box on the street would be better than a move back home to a mother she can't ever please, so she abandoned her tea and toast and scrolled the internet on her phone. Plenty of available apartments were close to school. She cringed at the price of rent and the square footage but set two appointments to walk through apartments after school the following day. Her mom was attending a luncheon while her dad tinkered in his wood shop, so Emma ran three miles around the neighborhood to clear her mind of the abrupt end of her marriage and her visions of a baby dashed.

. . .

"Rent doesn't include utilities. No pets allowed. You park on the street," said the landlord, who leaned against the door in a dirty shirt and pants. A cigarette dangled from his lips.

Emma ran her hand along the tiny counter in the kitchenette and groaned at the lack of a dishwasher. The bathroom sink had separate hot and cold faucets and rust stains. Storage in the studio apartment consisted of an umbrella closet and hooks behind the bathroom door. The astronomical rent for such a small place bordered on criminal, but school was two train stops away and a park was across the street.

"Lady? Do you want the place or not?"

Emma eyed the four locks on the door, but said, "Yep. I'll take it. Where do I sign?"

Craig rested his shoulder against the doorjamb as Emma tossed clothes from her side of the walk-in closet and dresser drawers into her luggage and boxes. "Why can't we talk about this? I messed up one time, I swear."

Emma squinted her eyes at Craig. His thick brown hair and hazel eyes still fluttered her heart, but the image of him with his assistant turned her stomach. "Seriously? You're going to stand there and tell me your assistant didn't join you for all those late 'working' nights and weekends?"

Craig avoided her gaze. "Well . . . what did you expect? You graded papers every night for school."

Emma shook her head and wagged her finger at him. "Oooh, no. Don't you dare throw school in my face. *You're* the one who cheated."

"Come on. The passion in our marriage ended years ago."

"Yeah, well, seven years of picking up your husband's dirty shorts off the floor sucks the passion right out of a marriage." She tossed her sweaters into a box and moved on to her bottom drawer. The skinny jeans, tight for five years, taunted her from the bottom of her dresser, but she threw them in the box anyway.

Craig crossed his arms and blew out a breath.

"I'll pick up the love seat and guest bed over the weekend. My lawyer will contact you." Emma lugged her suitcases and boxes down to her car, and then up the three flights of stairs to her new apartment.

Bins and boxes littered her apartment, and mounds of clothes dwarfed the small space. While she sat on the scuffed hardwood floor, she sorted piles to keep and to donate as she mulled over what Craig had said about passion. They'd experimented with a few toys, and she bought a silk nightie the first year of their marriage, but, after a few years, sex became a weekend chore. Craig preferred the missionary position with no foreplay. Their routine never faltered, even leading up to the weeks before she found him in the shower with his assistant. But the question poked at her. Did she and Craig ever have passion?

Weeks passed and she filled her dismal space with soft blue linens and multi-colored stoneware. A warm throw rug defined the area between her bed and the kitchenette. Her clothes were piled in the tiny closet and in clear bins under her bed. Shoes lived in a lower kitchen cabinet, and she covered the love seat with a slipcover to disguise the piece of furniture she'd shared with Craig. Her new home came together, and she started over.

Rain poured in sheets outside the sterile conference-room window six months later. Emma and her lawyer sat across from Craig and his attorney to sign the final dissolution of marriage. After she learned that Craig's affair started two years prior to the shower incident, she fought long and hard for her fair share of the settlement. Her daily runs along the lakeshore eased the stress associated with the divorce and the kids at school kept her busy and grounded. She stole glances at Craig in his designer suit and carefully styled hair and remembered how he'd swept her away with his attractive looks and smooth moves. Never again would she fall prey to such surface qualities in a man.

Chapter Two

"MRS. RICHARDS? Mrs. Richards, I don't feel so good."

Emma leaned down as a sweet little girl in her first-grade class tugged on her shirt.

"Mrs. Richards, I'm gonna . . ."

The girl bent over and threw up on Emma's shoes.

"Oh, sweetie, I'm sorry. Let's get you to the office."

Emma enlisted her teammate Jackie to watch her class finish the field-day activity and hustled the child inside PS 137. The old brick building lacked air conditioning and sweltered in the June heat as Emma escorted her student to the office. She settled her in a chair and set a garbage can beside her.

"We'll call your mom to pick you up."

"I'm gonna miss the popsicles," her student cried.

"It's okay, sweetheart. Today is the last day of school, and I'll make sure Mom has your popsicle to bring home."

She lifted her tiny head and alligator tears rimmed her eyes. Emma patted her on the shoulder. "Mom will be here soon."

Brown paper towels in the staff bathroom didn't clean all the vomit off Emma's shoes. She gathered the child's bookbag and popsicle from the classroom. She hugged her student goodbye and retreated to the lounge to join her teammates for lunch.

"Sick kid, Emma?" asked Jackie.

"Yep. I think the heat pushed her over the edge. It's oppressive out there and worse in the building. I've lost my appetite. She threw up on my shoes."

"Ick," said Alyssa.

"It's the worst thing about teaching," said Emma. She drank from her water bottle and breathed through her mouth to avoid the smell emanating from her shoes. "Hey, let's celebrate the end of school. Everyone free next weekend?"

"Why not this weekend?" asked Alyssa.

"My parents' annual barbecue is tomorrow."

"Fun." Jackie winked. "I bet your mom will criticize your hair."

"Nah, she'll be all up in your business about your love life," said Nicole.

"Truth," said Emma. "Let's try the new martini bar on Clark next Saturday."

"Perfect," said Jackie.

The last day of school ended with a clap-out to the fifth graders, and Emma wished her sticky brood a fun summer. She trudged the two blocks to the train station with her heavy teacher bag on her shoulder. The jam-packed Red Line jostled Emma against the throngs of people with heavy body odors, and she read an ad on the train wall. *A Northern Woods Adventure: Canoe in the Boundary Waters through the pristine wilderness.* The ad featured a beautiful blue lake and an emerald-green forest. The sun danced on the water's surface while four canoes drifted across the lake. She snapped a picture of the ad with her phone as a woman with a stroller banged into her shin. Emma winced, but smiled at the chubby toddler who sucked on a teething ring in the stroller.

The "oven," which doubled as her studio apartment, broiled on the hot June day, and she threw open the window to get a breeze. She stripped off her school clothes and stepped into her claw-foot tub for a cold shower. Her wet hair cooled her body while her laptop booted. She phoned in Thai food for dinner and grabbed a beer out of the fridge.

Cold beer in hand, Emma sat cross-legged on her bed and typed in the website from the ad on the train. Northern Woods featured canoeing through the Boundary Waters Canoe Area— the area in northern Minnesota next to the Canadian border. She scrolled through pictures of a large log cabin–style lodge with an expansive fireplace room, an open area for dining, and rocking chairs on a wraparound front porch. Guest rooms featured four-poster beds and en suites with jetted tubs. Picture windows in every room showcased views of the surrounding wilderness.

Her limited experience with vacations consisted of family trips to the ocean in a hotel with a pool and her disastrous honeymoon to Mexico. Craig planned the trip to a resort but neglected to inquire about safe drinking water. After three days on the hotel bathroom floor, Emma had begged to go home, and they never took another vacation. The woods and the lakes would be a new experience—maybe she'd give it a try.

The hot and humid weather continued to blanket the city the next day for her parents' annual neighborhood barbecue. She wore a cotton sundress and debated what to do with her hair. She settled on a ponytail with a ribbon to match her dress. The vanilla cake she bought from the corner market fit onto her own platter, and Emma sprinkled chocolate shavings on the top for a homemade touch. The dessert rested on the passenger seat of her Jeep. She missed her comfortable Lexus, but had traded it in after the divorce to save money. A downtown Chicago lifestyle on a teacher's salary challenged her bank account.

An hour later, Emma pulled up in front of her parents' suburban home. Cars filled the tree-lined street in front of the four-bedroom colonial, which was painted white with black shutters and a cherry-red front door. The spotless windows sparkled in the sun while flowers in perfect rows, like military soldiers in a parade, lined the front walk. The manicured lawn and a tasteful wreath on the front door welcomed guests, and conversation echoed from the backyard as she let herself into the house and found a space on the buffet for the cake. She headed out to the patio area where neighbors gathered near the pool and enjoyed drinks and appetizers. Smoke from the grill filled the air, and Emma poured herself a glass of white wine, but before she drank a drop, her mother and a neighbor invaded her space.

"You wore a wrinkled dress," her mom clucked.

She ignored her mom's insult and tried a different tactic. "Your flowers look great, Mom."

Her mom fingered her hair and tsked. "You need to get on top of those gray hairs. You're back on the market."

Emma pulled back from her mother's touch, and the neighbor asked, "Back on the market? What happened to Craig?"

"I walked in on him and his assistant in my bathroom." Emma took another sip of her wine. "In the shower." The neighbor's eyes widened, and Emma drank more wine. "Together." Emma gulped her wine as the neighbor gasped.

"Don't be crass, dear," said her mom.

"Our divorce became final in April." Emma drained her glass.

"You'll find another husband this summer." The neighbor snapped her fingers. "I know the perfect man at my church. He never misses a Sunday sermon and leads the Bible study group. He raises ferrets and competes in backgammon tournaments. He's perfect for you!"

Emma coughed and sputtered. "No, thank you." She turned back to her mother. "School is out for the summer. I said goodbye to another flock of kiddos, and I might go on a vacation."

"By yourself? It's not wise for a young woman to travel alone," said her mom.

Emma frowned at her empty wine glass. "I need some food and want to say hi to Dad." She escaped from her mom, poured herself a second glass of wine, and approached the grill.

Her dad welcomed her with an easy smile and a peck on the cheek. "Would you like a hamburger?"

"Sure, thanks." She stepped back and chuckled. "How're you allowed to wear an apron with the phrase 'The Grillfather' while I'm admonished for a wrinkle in my dress?"

"She worries about you."

"I don't think worry is the right word, but I'm fine. The divorce is final, and the school year is over."

"What are your summer plans?" asked her dad.

"I might take a vacation to the Boundary Waters in Minnesota."

Her dad nodded as he flipped the burgers. A fierce sizzle resulted and smoke curled up from the grill. "I think a vacation is an excellent idea. The Boundary Waters is a protected natural area, right?"

"Right." He loaded her plate and Emma settled into a patio chair while her mom worked the crowd and neighbors gossiped nearby. Conversations steered clear of politics and centered on the safe topics of children and grandchildren. She ate her hamburger and chit-chatted with a woman from down the street. Dinner drifted into dessert and neighbors left as the sun set.

After the guests departed, Emma put the leftover food in the refrigerator and wiped the kitchen counter. She folded the dish towel and returned to the patio where her parents' heads were pressed together over their laptop computer.

Her mom said, "Sit down, dear. We have news." Her mom folded her hands in her lap while Emma sat in the chair across from them. "We've purchased a home in a retirement community in Vero Beach. We'll move next month."

Emma swung her head back and forth from her mom to her dad. "Florida? Are you serious?"

Her dad raised his eyebrows and smiled. "We'll live close to the ocean. What do you think?" He turned the laptop to show Emma the pictures.

Emma, not interested in the website, flopped back in the chair and crossed her arms. "You've lived in the Chicago suburbs for thirty years. All of your friends are here!" She tilted her head and pulled her bottom lip. "*I'm* here."

Her mom shrugged. "What did you expect when you divorced our one chance for a grandchild?"

Emma's mouth fell open and her eyes narrowed. "That's low, Mom, even for you." Emma pulled her keys from her purse. "I'm outta here."

Her dad's voice floated in the warm night air as she walked to her car. "Why do you antagonize her?"

"I state the facts."

"You drive her away."

Emma paused on the side of the house to listen.

"She creates her own messes. Remember the man she dated

13

from California who majored in entertainment technology and wore cut-off jeans? Cut-off jeans are not appropriate attire at my dinner table. What was she thinking? But then she brought home perfect Craig. He majored in business and drove a Mercedes! The expensive bottle of wine he brought to our first dinner together was delicious, *and* he wore a tailored suit to my table. I worked hard to convince Emma that Craig, the only son of a wealthy family—and our ticket into Chicago's elite clubs—was perfect for her. Remember the *perfect* wedding? The girls at the club talked about that wedding for months. Seven years—where's my grandchild?"

"First of all, who cares what some guy wore to our dinner table a million years ago? And the wedding? I remember Emma cried when Craig got drunk at the reception and flirted with a server. And I hate that pretentious club. A baby? It takes two to get pregnant, and Craig was busy with his affair. Besides, Emma doesn't need to be married or have a baby to be successful. She's an accomplished schoolteacher."

"Oh, *puh*-lease. Anyone with a pulse can look after a group of six-year-olds."

Her dad's voice sharpened. "Emma works hard at her career. She earned a master's degree and won teacher of the year at her school two years ago!"

"I wanted to show off a baby to the girls at the club, but now . . ."

"He *cheated*," her dad yelled, and the noise bounced off the side of the house.

"Well, why do you suppose he cheated? There are two sides to every story."

"Yes, but I wish you'd take the side of our only child once in a while."

Tears gathered in Emma's eyes, and she jumped when the patio door slammed. Her dad always defended her, but her mom's question continued to plague her months after the divorce. Why *did* Craig cheat?

After she fought the busy Saturday night traffic, Emma parked her Jeep in the first spot she located—two blocks from her apartment—and walked to her building. She passed a couple in the dank hallway in a tight embrace. The young woman clenched her leg around the guy's thigh as he fondled her breast through her tank top with one hand and fiddled with the key in the door with his other hand. Her long hair obscured their intense lip lock, and their moans echoed in the hallway. Emma scrambled past them, and her hands shook as she worked her locks. She slammed the door and leaned her body against it. The erotic noises from the couple sparked envy in her. Was it possible to love another person so much you couldn't even wait to get through the door?

A hot, restless night followed the barbecue, and Emma gave up on sleep and hauled herself out of bed. She laced up her running shoes and headed to the park. Her ponytail bounced as she ran three miles up the lakeshore and battled the incessant wind on the way back home. Sweat poured off her body and her lungs burned as she stretched her tight Achilles. Emma showered, and then she booted up her laptop to continue the research on a vacation to Northern Woods. Suddenly, her phone rang.

"What day will you work in your room at school next week?" asked her teammate Nicole.

"Thursday or Friday. Why?" asked Emma.

"I've got your math materials."

"No problem. Toss them into my supply closet. Hey, what do you know about canoeing?"

Nicole's voice dropped a level. "Not much, but . . . sex in a canoe is fantastic. The rocking is phenomenal. Of course, my husband and I have spectacular sex in lots of places."

Nicole's sex stories rivaled the steamy romance novels Emma devoured. "I don't think spectacular sex is for me."

"Everyone deserves spectacular sex. See you next week."

The computer scrolled through pictures of birds, lakes, and old men fishing in northern Minnesota. A vacation to Northern Woods wouldn't result in spectacular sex, since old men in flannel shirts didn't kickstart her libido. She surfed the internet for Caribbean resorts for the next hour, but memories of spring breaks popped into her head, and she didn't want a repeat of the college scene. Spectacular sex could wait until she found a suitable mate in Chicago.

The following Saturday, Emma plowed through the jumbles of clothes in her closet for an outfit to wear for the girls' night out. She dismissed sundresses and teacher outfits and wrestled into a black miniskirt and a blousy cream-colored top. Sandals uncomfortable enough to look sexy adorned her feet, and she curled her hair.

Jackie screeched up to the curb in her compact car dressed in a strapless sheath, her dirty-blond hair in an updo. "Nicole and Alyssa will meet us at the bar. Nicole struggled to find a sitter, but a neighbor filled in for . . ." Jackie glanced at Emma as she stared out the window. "Are you okay?"

"I'm fine," replied Emma. "I need to get out of this city. I might go on vacation."

Jackie shrugged and navigated her car through the traffic. They pulled up to the valet, and then strolled into the hazy bar.

Music thumped, lights flashed to the beat, and men and women sized one another up on the dance floor. Nicole and Alyssa waved them over to their table.

"Isn't this place great?" Alyssa asked.

The friends ordered drinks and an appetizer to share. They gossiped about teachers at school until conversation drifted to their personal lives.

"So, where do you want to go on vacation, Emma?" asked Jackie.

Emma sipped her cosmo. "The Boundary Waters."

"What's the Boundary Waters?" asked Nicole.

"It's a collection of lakes on the northern border of Minnesota. There's a gorgeous lodge with this cool porch. I want to learn how to canoe."

"You deserve a vacation," said Alyssa.

"Sounds perfect. Let's dance," said Jackie.

The friends danced and Emma flirted with a tall blond from across the dance floor. He sauntered over to her and took her hand without a word. She turned and smiled at her girlfriends, then followed him to a quieter corner of the club. He introduced himself and bought her a drink before they danced. His sexy grin and white-blond hair contributed to his handsomeness and his dance moves made her belly flutter inside.

"Care to go somewhere quieter? I live around the corner."

Emma bit her bottom lip and pondered the situation. A night with a sexy man would trump the usual, single-handed pleasure she'd resorted to after the divorce slammed the door on her sex life. But her brain screamed at her not to trust the hot guy. In the end, her alcohol-fueled libido overruled her brain cells. "Sure. Let me tell my girlfriends."

Emma weaved her way back to the other side of the bar. "Hey, I'm headed out with this guy," she shouted to her friends over the din.

Nicole winked. "You go, girl. Call if you need us."

Emma smiled and waved goodbye to her friends.

Heat, humidity, exhaust fumes, and greasy smells from restaurants hung in the midnight air as they strolled down the street holding hands. He guided her into a well-appointed brownstone. She slipped off her sandals inside the door.

"Make yourself at home. I'll pour us a glass of wine."

Her toes squished in the deep pile rug, and she ran her hand along the back of a buttery leather couch. A flatscreen TV bigger than her kitchen table perched on one wall and a piece of modern art graced the opposite wall in the beautiful home. He approached with two glasses of wine and hit a button on a remote. The lights dimmed and quiet jazz played. She sipped her wine and gazed into eyes as green as grass. He set her wineglass on a table and eased her into his arms. They swayed to the music and picked up where they'd left off at the club. He bent down and kissed her neck and cheek. A tiny zing flew through her belly. She offered him her lips, and he brushed his against them. Emma garnered self-confidence and opened her mouth to him as he worked the buttons on her blouse. Her hands traveled under his shirt, where she found sculpted muscles and a smooth chest. As her blouse hit the ground, his phone buzzed in his back pocket. He pulled it out and swiped the screen.

"Hey," he said into the phone. "Yeah. It's poker night with the guys."

Emma stilled. *Poker?*

"Tomorrow? Sure. I'll pick you up around ten."

He hung up the phone.

"Poker with the guys?" asked Emma.

He snaked his hand up her arm and slid her bra strap off her shoulder to expose her right breast. "A little white lie. She'll never know."

Emma pulled back and replaced her bra strap. "*Who* will never know? Who called you?"

He ran a hand through his wavy hair and sighed. "My fiancé, okay? Brunch with her parents isn't until eleven. We've got all night."

Emma blanched. "Fiancé? You're a jackass."

"What? It's not like we're married."

"I'm outta here." Emma grabbed her blouse and threw it on, slipped into her shoes, and tore out of the apartment.

"Wait!" he called, but she flew down the steps into the hot night.

She buttoned her blouse and hailed a taxi on the corner. Safe in the car, she exhaled and leaned her head back on the leather seat.

"You all right, miss?" asked the taxi driver.

"How come every attractive guy in this city is a complete and utter asshole?"

The taxi driver peered at her in his rearview mirror and chuckled.

Chapter Three

THE MORNING after the club debacle, Emma returned to her laptop and longed for the quiet peacefulness of northern Minnesota. The constant street noise of cars and sirens hammered her soul. She imagined herself with a book on the porch of the lodge or in a canoe on the lake. The peaceful setting called to her after her hellacious year.

She brought up the registration page, typed in the required information, and had just entered her credit card number when a knock at her door interrupted the process. "Hang on," she called.

Emma opened her door to Craig and recoiled. "What do you want?"

"Can we talk?" asked Craig.

"No." She attempted to slam the door, but Craig slipped his hand inside the jamb.

"Wait. Please? Can I come in?"

Emma opened the door but didn't let Craig beyond the threshold. She crossed her arms and waited for him to speak.

Craig stood in the doorway of her studio apartment in trendy clothes, shifting his weight from foot to foot. "I . . . well . . . um . . . my assistant is pregnant. I didn't want you to hear it from anyone else."

Emma's mouth opened but silence hung in the air between them. "Get. Out." She put her hand on the door, and Craig left without another word.

She slammed the door and flopped down on her bed, tears in her eyes. Pregnant? Craig had rejected every attempt she'd made to try for a baby. He would always say, "A baby? You look after kids every day. We don't need a baby." She would answer, "I teach children at school. I don't raise them. I want a baby." And he would say, "Not yet," or "We're too busy."

Well, screw him. She wiped away her tears and hit the submit button—and booked a two-week trip to the Boundary Waters in late June.

An hour later, Emma received a confirmation email from Northern Woods with reminders to pack light and to bring a sleeping bag and dry pack. Confused, she reread the communication as sweat beaded on her upper lip. Why would she need a sleeping bag to sleep in a four-poster bed in a lodge? She reviewed the confirmation email, her heart nearly beating out of her chest. She'd paid for a guided canoe camping trip through the Boundary Waters, not a two-week stay in a beautiful lodge. Shit, shit, *shit*. Northern Woods would refund her registration fee, but she would lose the rest of her money if she canceled now. She picked up her phone and dialed Jackie.

"I've made a terrible mistake."

"You shouldn't have left with that blond guy. Where are you? I'll pick you up."

"No, no, no. I'll tell you about him another time. My trip. I .
. . um . . . I signed up for a two-week guided canoe camping trip
by accident."

Jackie laughed into the phone, and Emma rolled her eyes.
Her friend had helped her escape from a myriad of troubles
since their college days; one time, when she'd almost missed an
exam after a drunken night at a fraternity house, and another
time, when she'd slept in a library on campus overnight. Jackie
had saved her butt tons of times.

"Help me."

"Are you going on the trip?"

"I already paid the money, and I would lose a huge portion
of it if I canceled, so yeah, I guess I'm camping for my
vacation."

"Well, since you've never camped a day in your life, I
suggest a trip to the store for the basics. I'll pick you up at ten."

Aisle after aisle after aisle of camping supplies knotted Emma's
stomach. She'd quit the Girl Scouts after third grade and didn't
remember a thing from it. The items available for camp cooking
alone filled three aisles. Jackie had worked every summer
during college at a residential Y camp and insisted she buy the
highest-quality sleeping bag and a rubber pouch to hold her
clothes.

"Wouldn't a suitcase with wheels be easier than this rubber
sack?" Emma wrinkled her nose. The pouch smelled fishy, and
she didn't think it would fit all her clothes.

"Your clothes need to stay dry in a canoe. Your luggage is
perfect for an airport, but not the woods. Come on, you need
rain gear and high-quality hiking boots."

Emma cradled her jumpy stomach. "I can't sleep on the

ground. What about bathrooms and showers? I can't survive without a hair dryer for two weeks."

"It's your decision, but camping is pretty awesome. You'll see some great scenery and animals. Quality gear will keep you as comfortable as possible."

Emma fingered a stack of multicolored shorts. "Well, these shorts *are* pretty cute."

They piled gear into a cart for the next several hours, and Emma's credit card took a big hit at checkout.

Jackie idled her car in front of Emma's apartment. "Wear the hiking boots around to break them in before your trip. Trust me. You'll thank me later."

"Got it," said Emma as she hugged her friend goodbye.

"See you soon." Jackie drove away from the curb and left Emma to lug her gear up to her apartment alone.

Emma tried on her new clothes and walked around her apartment in her hiking boots. She tossed her hair over her shoulder and rested one hand on her hip. She shook her head in the mirror. Who was she kidding? A born and bred city girl would never survive two weeks on the lakes in the Boundary Waters.

Emma shared a meal with her parents the following weekend. They'd transformed their home into a staged house, and labeled boxes littered the rooms. One lone box with her name on it sat by the door, ready for her to take back to her apartment.

"One box? One box from the stack in my bedroom closet?"

"I tossed the junk and sold your violin. Anything important is in that box."

Emma shook her head. "When does the real-estate sign go up in the yard?"

"Monday," replied her dad. "The realtor told us several interested buyers will walk through on Tuesday. We'll move these boxes to the basement tomorrow. We're exhausted after today. The truck arrives next week."

"I'm sure you'll sell fast. This is a great neighborhood." A moment of nostalgia hit Emma, and she sighed at all the changes.

"When do you leave for your vacation?" asked her dad.

"The day after tomorrow. I'll catch a shuttle in Duluth to ride to the lodge." Emma left out the minor detail of the ten-day canoeing and camping adventure through the Minnesota wilderness. Her mother didn't need additional ammunition about Emma's screw-ups in life.

"A lodge? Doesn't Minnesota have decent hotels?" asked her mom.

"The lodge looks fine."

"Does it even have a pool?"

"I don't think so."

Emma's mom pursed her lips and shook her head. "A disgrace."

Emma choked a bit on her piece of chicken and wiped her mouth. "I'll survive."

Her mom yammered on throughout the meal, describing their new home, the development, and the activities available there. She recounted the details of the move and elaborated on the debate over what size golf cart to purchase.

After dessert, Emma's dad loaded the box into the back seat of her Jeep and held the door open for her as her mom stood back. "Be careful on the drive to Minnesota and enjoy your vacation," said her dad.

"Thanks. I'll call you in Florida when I get home." She hugged her dad hard, and he brushed a tear from her cheek when they parted.

Her mom cleared her throat. "Visit soon, dear." Emma received her mom's air kiss and slid into her Jeep, and her dad closed the door. She backed out of the driveway and waved at their silhouettes in the moonlight.

The early morning sun streamed through her window. Emma rolled over in bed to a cool spot on the sheet. Unable to go back to sleep, her eyes settled on the unopened box she'd left on her table the previous night. Curious, she padded across her apartment and ripped open the packaging tape. She pulled out trophies and medals, and she was leafing through the pictures when a small, hardbound, blue book with gems on its cover peeked at her from the bottom of the box. The last time she'd written in her teenage diary was a dozen years ago, and she yelped with glee at the find. She rifled through papers and books, but the key to her diary was not in the box, so Emma grabbed a steak knife and broke the lock. She flopped back on her bed and paged through the book.

The loopy teen script highlighted highs and lows from high school. She read impressive details from her first kiss, behind the football bleachers. A poor grade on a biology test plagued her in November of her sophomore year. A mean girl teased her about her flat chest in the gym locker room, and she giggled when she read about a make-out session with a guy senior year while they shared a wine cooler in his truck. She fanned her face from her descriptions of teen love steaming up the truck windows. Gripes about her mother flowed throughout the diary, and Emma shook her head at their failed relationship. There were pages filled with her dreams to attend college out west and study in Europe. She sighed. She'd chosen the safe, in-state college and spring break trips to Florida. A study abroad program to Italy piqued her interest junior year of college, but her mother had convinced her not to apply, fearing Craig might break up with her if she left campus for a semester. Her unfulfilled wanderlust fueled her excitement about the trip to Northern Woods. It wasn't Europe, but it was a start.

Chapter Four

THE NEW RUBBER SACK, stuffed with her clothes and her sleeping bag, sat on the back seat in her Jeep. Her suitcase, filled with extra clothes, fit into the back. Dressed in a new pair of camp shorts, a T-shirt to match, and the hiking boots, she drove north to Duluth. The sun rose over Lake Michigan as her hair flapped in the breeze from the open window and she sang along with the radio. She envisioned a hike on a beautiful trail in her new clothes and boots. Fifteen miles later, she stopped at a rest stop and yanked the heavy boots off her feet. Thankful she'd packed her flip-flops, she slipped them on and continued on her way.

The traffic thinned through Wisconsin, and she stopped for a fast-food lunch in a small town. A cooler temperature greeted her as she stretched and filled her gas tank in Eau Claire. A teenage couple filled theirs at the next pump.

"I'm not sure about the bonfire," said the girl, who wore a crop top and cowboy boots.

"It'll be great," said the guy.

"You'll stay with me, right?"

"You bet." The guy sidled up to the girl and slid his hand along her bare midriff.

The girl nuzzled into his shoulder while he peered at Emma, raised an eyebrow, and winked.

Emma grimaced and returned her nozzle to the pump.

"You're so good to me," said the girl.

Emma groaned. Jerks lived *everywhere*.

The two-lane highway to Duluth featured dense forest on both sides of the road. The prolific roadkill nauseated her, and bugs of all shapes and sizes found their deaths on her windshield. Emma parked her car in downtown Duluth. She checked her watch: three o'clock. The lodge van picked the guests up from the local bus station at five. A snack would tide her over until she arrived at the lodge. She spied a cafe on the other side of a park.

A stiff breeze blew, but the sun warmed her. People jogged, and children laughed and shouted while they played on the playground in the park. She passed a young family with a kite in the grassy field and smiled at the toddler's shouts of joy as it lifted into the air.

Bells jingled as she pushed open the heavy door of the busy cafe. The barista filled her order of iced tea and a blueberry scone, and Emma left a generous tip for the teenager. She turned to find a table, but instead slammed into a solid wall of man. The scone flew out of her hand, and the cold tea spilled down her new clothes.

"Damn it." Emma reached behind her to grab a paper napkin from the counter.

The man jumped backward and said, "I'll call you back" to the person on the phone and "I'm so sorry" to Emma.

Emma brushed her shirt with the napkin and stepped away from the tea pooled around her flip-flops.

"I'll buy you another drink. I'm so sorry. I didn't see you."

Emma picked up the empty cup and the scone from the ground and scowled at him. She tossed both in the trash and headed out the door.

"Wait!" The guy followed her outside and touched her elbow. "Let me buy you another drink, please."

Emma was startled by the soft touch of the broad man. His sizable hand engulfed her elbow, warming her arm. She paused, oddly comforted by the stranger's touch, but then gathered her wits and shook off his hand.

"No, thanks." She walked away as his eyes bored into her back.

Chapter Five

Mark dressed in the requisite suit and tie for his job at a large CPA firm in downtown Minneapolis. He greeted his assistant and picked up his messages outside his office. "Did you have a nice weekend?" asked Mark.

His assistant, a forty-year-old mom of two, glanced up from her computer with a surprised smile. "I had a great weekend. Thanks. What did you do this weekend?"

"I went camping with a friend, and I loved it so much I might buy a canoe or a kayak."

"Great idea." She regarded Mark and folded her hands in her lap. "Sir, if you don't mind me saying so, it's nice to see you smile."

His lips curved. "Thanks."

He walked into his office and set his briefcase on the desk. He opened the blinds on the window and waited for his computer to boot up. The view of downtown Minneapolis from his window paled in comparison to the woods.

His best buddy, Rick, had asked him to go camping and he'd dreaded the trip. But the first morning, when Mark unzipped the tent and walked to the shore, a weight lifted. The clear blue lake reflected the sun and small waves lapped at the rocks. A subtle breeze from the trees gently blew his T-shirt.

Rick approached him. "Cool, isn't it?"

"Yeah, it's awesome. The lake is smooth, like glass. It's so peaceful."

Rick taught him the basics of how to fish, but otherwise left him alone. Mark listened to the loons and hiked in the woods. He stared into the flames of the campfire at night. His mind cleared, and he breathed the clean air and relished the quiet.

A few weeks later, Mark purchased a tent and a sleeping bag. His first solo camping trip tried his patience with several near disasters, but as the summer progressed, Mark improved his skills and bought a canoe. He learned how to hoist the canoe on top of his Tahoe and expanded his explorations. Camping provided him with the time and space to grieve and a sense of peace that comforted him like a warm blanket. He took long walks in the woods and learned how to fish. He taught himself how to identify birds and read the stars on different lakes all over Minnesota.

The following spring, flipping through a camping magazine, he came across an ad for Northern Woods. It boasted a two-week canoe camping trip through the Boundary Waters in northern Minnesota. Mark loved camping but had never canoed from lake to lake. After further research, he booked the ten-day adventure.

One night, when he and Rick grabbed a beer after work, he told him about it.

"It sounds like a cool trip," said Rick. "You love to camp, and it's a challenge to canoe from lake to lake."

"Tax season is over, and summer is my downtime."

"Sounds great. The lodge looks cool, and the scenery is awesome." Rick took a long pull on his beer. "Maybe you'll meet someone."

The noise of the bar melted away as images of Meg flickered through his mind, and he twisted the wedding ring on his finger. Any reminder of the loss of his wife triggered his grief. He'd struggled with daily life in the weeks after her death. The pain had consumed him and when he almost broke for good, Rick had suggested the first camping trip, and nature clicked him back into reality. Since then, Mark spent all his free time in the woods—an activity Meg never would have tried.

"She passed away over a year ago, but it seems like yesterday." Rick nodded.

Mark drank the last of his beer and set his bottle on the table with a sigh. "Camping helped me deal with the grief."

"When do you leave?" asked Rick.

"The end of June. I'll drive to Duluth and meet a shuttle that transports guests to the lodge."

"Perfect. The Boundary Waters is awesome. I can't wait to hear all about it."

Mark removed his wedding band and placed it on his bedside table the morning he left for Northern Woods. He rubbed the bare skin and stared at the ring but left it on the nightstand. He didn't want to lose it on the long canoe trip. The easy drive to Duluth allowed him time for a bite to eat before the shuttles arrived, and a cafe sat on the edge of a park. He was walking through the park, around soccer games, when his phone rang.

He smiled at the screen. "Hey Rick."

"Got a second? My bank charged me an outrageous fee and I need some advice."

"Read me the letter."

He listened to Rick on the phone and pushed the heavy cafe door open. A warm, yeasty smell greeted him. He barreled toward the counter but stopped short when a small woman slammed into him. "I'll call you back."

The woman, dressed in short-shorts and flip-flops, her hair in a ponytail, spilled her drink all over herself when she walked into his chest. Her scone flew through the air, and he had to stifle a laugh as she attempted to wipe the iced tea from her shirt.

She tossed her food into the trash and headed outside. "I'm so sorry," he called to her. He ran after her and touched her arm to stop her. "Let me buy you another drink, please." The warmth of her body radiated through his fingertips and zinged up his arm. She held his gaze for a minute, but then shrugged off his grip, said no, and walked away. Mark rubbed his hand, and his eyes followed the small woman as she moved through the park. Her ponytail swung from side to side, and he couldn't help but notice how her waist narrowed into slim hips on top of sculpted legs.

He called Rick back. "What the hell?" asked Rick.

"I ran into a woman in a cafe and spilled her drink. I offered to buy her a new one, but she walked away."

"Smooth."

"Listen, I need to go. Contact your bank and challenge the fee. I'll call you in two weeks."

Mark ate his sandwich and gulped down his coffee while he drove to the bus station. He tossed his trash and gathered his gear. An eclectic group of people waited in the gravel lot for the shuttles up to the lodge—including the woman who spilled her tea at the cafe. He locked eyes with her and curled his lips into a smile as she muttered, "Damn."

White shuttles with the blue Northern Woods logo pulled into the lot at five o'clock.

He loaded his gear onto the first shuttle, took a seat beside an older woman with snow-white hair and extended his hand. "Mark."

She shook it. "Helen."

"First trip?" he asked.

"Tenth." She inserted earbuds, and Mark nodded his acceptance and turned his attention to the scenery out the window on the way up to the lodge.

Chapter Six

EMMA LUGGED her gear onto the second van, added it to the pile in the back, and found a seat near the middle. Out the window, the guy who'd slammed into her and spilled her tea at the cafe boarded the first shuttle. She rolled her eyes and averted her gaze from his broad shoulders and chiseled jaw. The heavy backpack slipped off her shoulders and she held it on her lap. Guests included men, women, a few college kids, a woman with snow-white hair who dwarfed the majority of the men, and the guy from the cafe. A woman dressed in a designer skirt and heels with a matched set of suitcases struggled to walk across the gravel lot.

Meanwhile, a tall girl with long, red, curly hair approached Emma.

"Hey, can I sit with you?" she asked.

"Sure. I'm Emma."

The girl flopped down on the seat beside Emma. "I'm Penny. Those are kickass hiking boots and cute shorts."

Emma nodded her head. "Thanks. My friend helped me shop. The clothes are all brand new."

"My parents gave me this trip for my birthday. How did you wind up here?"

"My summers are free, and I needed a break from the city—Chicago." Emma lowered her voice and continued. "I booked a trip to a gorgeous lodge to relax and canoe in the afternoons. After I'd paid the money, I discovered I'd signed up for a ten-day canoe camping trip through the wilderness. I'm clueless."

Penny smirked. "You're in for an adventure."

"This is my first time camping."

Penny nodded. "I've camped dozens of times, but never over the lakes. My family camping memories are awesome."

"Where're you from?" asked Emma.

"Rochester, Minnesota. I'm a junior at a small music school in Minnesota."

"You look too young to be in college."

"I'm twenty. Are you in college?"

Emma smirked. "No. But thanks. I'm twenty-nine."

Their easy banter continued for the duration of the ride to Northern Woods. Emma learned that Penny had broken up with her steady boyfriend a few weeks ago. She was the youngest of four kids and the only girl in her family. The roads narrowed to two lanes as they drove farther from Duluth. Dense forest dominated the landscape, and they passed a moose-crossing sign. Cars sped past with canoes or kayaks strapped to their roofs. SUVs hauled boats and trailers carried ATVs. Steady traffic littered the two-lane road. As they approached Ely, one- and two-story buildings came into view. They slowed through the town, which boasted a few hotels, family restaurants, camping stores, a library, a gas station, a grocer, and a sign for a school. Residents and tourists dined, window shopped, and enjoyed the beautiful evening in the tiny city.

The vans drove through an even smaller town with one

blinking stop light and turned left onto a dirt road. Penny's breasts bounced with each pothole they hit on the dirt road. Emma glanced down at her own small, motionless breasts, rolled her eyes, and focused on the scenery out the window. They bumped along until a Northern Woods sign came into view. The shuttles pulled up to the lodge. Built on a hilltop enveloped by pine trees, the large, log cabin–style lodge featured a main entrance with a wraparound front porch and a three-story annex, which housed the guest rooms offered after the trip. They exited the vans and waited for instructions. Emma inhaled a deep breath, and clean air filled her lungs. She avoided the man who'd spilled her tea, but his midnight-blue eyes followed her everywhere.

"Welcome to Northern Woods," said a woman dressed in khaki shorts and a blue polo shirt with the lodge logo. "Please store your luggage in the cabin and return to the lodge for dinner."

Emma and Penny unloaded their gear from the van and followed other guests to the women's cabin. The cavernous room held twelve bunk beds. A single lightbulb, hung from the ceiling, bathed the room in yellow. A small window with a dirty sill lacked blinds, and the white, metal bunk beds held razor-thin mattresses. She set her dry pack and sleeping bag on a lower bunk and turned around.

"Need a bathroom?" asked the older woman with white hair.

"Yep," replied Emma.

"The bathhouse is beyond the trees." She winked. "Enjoy it while you can."

Emma cringed. She didn't want to think about the bathroom facilities for the next two weeks. Instead, she trooped outside to check out the bathhouse. Sticks and rocks littered the path, and she stepped with care to avoid twisting an ankle. She pushed open a screen door, and it snapped back with a bang. Emma eyed sinks, toilets, and two shower heads. Flimsy shower curtains offered a modicum of privacy, and daddy longlegs climbed the walls. She wrinkled her nose at the musty smell, and she slipped on the wet cement floor. The sink water ran cold, but she washed her hands and ran her fingers through her hair.

Upon her return to the cabin, Emma sat on her bunk with her arms wrapped around her stomach.

"Are you sick?" asked Penny.

"Nervous and nauseous. Two weeks is forever in the wilderness."

Penny nodded. "One day at a time."

The two women hiked up the hill to the lodge. They walked through the lobby and past a room with a stone fireplace and chairs and couches to the enormous dining room, which featured a large picture window with a view of the lake. Photographs of the Boundary Waters covered the walls, and canoe paddles hung over the door. They joined the back of the line at the small buffet.

The woman who'd welcomed them stood and garnered their attention. "You traveled all day and are eager to settle into your cabins. Jim will pass out the agendas. Training for new guests begins at eight o'clock tomorrow morning. As usual, if you're a returning guest, you may enjoy the lodge and amenities for the next few days. If you need help, alert one of the staff. Sleep well, and we'll see you in the morning."

Emma reviewed the training agenda after the spaghetti and meatball dinner, and flinched when a chair scraped the floor. The man she'd run into at the cafe sat down beside her.

"Hey, I'm Mark. Sorry again for our collision at the cafe."

"I'm Emma. It's all right. I survived." Their eyes locked, and the deep blue color of his entranced her. His black hair, with a hint of silver at his sideburns, and square jaw made her chest feel fluttery.

She shook her head. Nope. She came to Northern Woods to learn how to canoe, not flirt with an attractive guy. "G'night." Emma grabbed her agenda and headed out the lodge's front door.

Full and exhausted, Emma sat on her bunk and pulled out her phone to text her friends. The woman with the snow-white hair said, "Sweetie, you need to go back to Ely to get a cell phone signal. You won't need your phone on the trip. I'm Helen, and I've traveled with Northern Woods for ten years. You picked a wonderful trip, but pay attention during training. Focus on acquiring the skills, and give your social media accounts a break. Your friends will understand. Tomorrow will be a long day, and you need to be well-rested to stay alert in the woods." Helen's heavy footfalls shook the cabin as she left to use the bathhouse.

"I don't think I've ever met such a large woman. Where do you think she buys clothes that fit her shoulders? And why is she so bossy?" asked Penny.

"Shh," said Emma. "Don't piss her off. She's experienced and we'll need her help later."

The women took turns in the bathhouse. Emma pulled on her pajamas and brushed her teeth. She climbed into her slippery sleeping bag and folded a sweatshirt for a pillow. The uncomfortable, thin mattress paled in comparison to her bed at home, but exhaustion won, and she drifted off to sleep.

Emma woke with a start to an unfamiliar noise. The eerie sound echoed through the dark cabin. Emma listened. The long wail repeated itself. She leaned over and whispered to Penny.

"Penny, wake up." Penny didn't move. Emma shook her arm and said louder, "Wake up."

"What's the matter?" Penny rubbed her eyes and blinked at Emma.

"Listen."

Penny listened. "Go back to sleep. It's the middle of the night."

She shook Penny again. "What's that noise?"

"A loon," Penny whispered.

"What?"

"It's a *loon*."

"A what?"

"It's a bird!" Penny yelled.

The rest of the women woke up—thanks to Penny's shrill voice.

Emma blushed. "Sorry." She slithered deep into her sleeping bag and slept off her embarrassment.

A cool morning brought a thick mist over the lake and dewy ground. Emma slipped on some clothes and headed to the lodge with Penny for waffles and sausage. Conversation bounced off the pine walls and echoed in the cavernous room. Mark and Helen shared a table, and Emma's brain warned her not to gawk, but Mark's broad frame and gorgeous eyes pulled at her like a magnet. She blushed when Mark caught her eye and winked.

After breakfast, Emma descended the hill from the lodge to the lakeshore. Her breath hitched as she absorbed the scenery. An emerald-green forest circled the property, and the lake—as blue as the sky—stretched out forever. Pictures of this very scene had drawn her to this part of the country, and her heartbeat slowed as she inhaled deep breaths of pine-scented air.

Canoes of different colors lay on a small beach, and the sun rose over the water and reflected the pine trees in the lake. The cacophony of birds who inhabited the forest entertained her as she waited for instruction.

The eight guests new to Northern Woods were Penny, Emma, fancy-luggage girl, and five men between the ages of twenty-five and sixty, including Mark. Four canoes rested against the shore, and different-sized paddles leaned against a tree. Jim, the training-session leader, worked as a guide for Northern Woods. He explained the front of the canoe—the bow—controlled the power and speed. The back of the canoe—the stern—steered the canoe. He taught the group how to hold a paddle, how to adjust it to steer the canoe, and he claimed that even very slight motions could change the canoe's direction.

Emma doubted such a small movement would change the large canoe's direction, but, always an obedient student, she followed Jim's instructions on land as they paddled air.

Satisfied with the group's progress, Jim distributed life jackets to everyone, regardless of swimming ability. Emma snapped her life jacket clips and grabbed her paddle.

"Partners? The blue canoe?" asked Penny.

Emma nodded. Penny wanted the bow, which meant that Emma would steer their canoe from the stern. They waited their turn as other couples got situated. Jim held onto the canoe's side as Penny stepped in and rocked the canoe back and forth. Jim steadied the canoe, and Emma climbed in. Once seated, he shoved them into the lake. Penny paddled on the left side, while Emma paddled on the right. Jim had suggested they switch from time to time. She drew another stroke, and they moved right again. Emma switched sides. They moved left and straightened out. Emma switched sides again and splashed water into the canoe. Her arms tired and frustration mounted. Several other guests struggled as well. One couple capsized their canoe and scrambled out of the water. Another pair shouted to each other as they spun in circles.

Mark and another man paddled toward them. "Turn your paddle in the water to steer the canoe. Like this." Mark showed her what he meant, and Emma nodded.

She pulled her paddle through the water and turned it counterclockwise. They canoed straight for the first time.

"It worked!" Penny turned around and gave her a thumbs-up. "Do it again." Emma pulled with her paddle, then corrected the course. She repeated her action as Penny whipped around and said, "We've got it!"

Emma thanked Mark as he and his partner paddled away. Jim pumped his fist from shore and cupped his hands over his mouth to yell, "Way to go, ladies!" They paddled around for an hour, experimenting with different sides and timing. Emma broke a sweat from the focus and strength needed to paddle the canoe but welcomed the lake's vast openness, a welcome shift from the crowded trains at home.

Penny turned around in the bow. "The handsome dude in the red canoe can't keep his eyes off you."

"His name is Mark and don't stare back," answered Emma.

"It's a shame he's old. He's buff," said Penny.

"He's not old—he's probably in his thirties—but he *is* the definition of buff."

"Thirties is old for me."

Emma concentrated on her new skills until Jim corralled them back to shore. Emma and Penny exited the canoe, pulled the heavy boat onto shore, and rested the paddles against a tree.

Mark heaved his canoe out of the water, and her eyes followed his well-defined calf muscles up to his thick thighs and filled-out shorts. Reality kicked in, and she turned back to the group.

Penny asked a question. "What's a portage?"

"We move the canoes and gear through the forest from one lake to the next," answered Jim. "The canoe balances on your shoulders as you walk the trail."

"Wait, what?" asked Emma. "Carry a canoe on our shoulders? Are you serious?"

"You betcha. We move from lake to lake along trails in the woods."

Emma and Penny exchanged wide-eyed glances. *Oh boy.* Did either of them have the strength to portage a canoe?

"I'm out," said the woman with the fancy luggage and designer clothes.

"Me too," said a guy with a gut and a heavy beard. "I'm not lugging a canoe through the woods. I wanted to fish and drink beer, not exercise."

The two disgruntled guests headed to the cabins to retrieve their gear and leave Northern Woods. Unphased by the two departures, Jim said, "We'll practice the portage after lunch. Nice work, everyone."

The wooden rocker creaked under Emma's weight, and a chipmunk scurried under the lodge's front porch. The dense forest and expansive lake contrasted with the concrete jungle at home. She didn't miss the horns and sirens, and the birds and woodland animals chittered and kept her company on the porch. A squirrel jumped onto the decking and stared at her but scampered away when the front door to the lodge opened. Mark sat down in the rocking chair beside her.

"You did great with the canoe," said Mark.

"Thanks. I've never canoed or camped before."

"I know."

Emma bit her bottom lip and faced Mark. "How can you tell?"

"All of your gear is brand new. If I were a betting man, I'd say your new hiking boots rub your ankles a tad."

Her new boots killed her. How did he know? Jackie had warned her to break them in, but she'd never worn them outside her apartment.

"Isn't it great up here? I love to camp, but this is my first time in the Boundary Waters," said Mark.

"It's different from Chicago." They rocked in silence. "Does your wife like to canoe or camp?" asked Emma.

"I'm not . . . I'm a . . . hey, I think I hear Helen. I'm gonna head to the lakeshore. See ya later." Mark stepped off the porch, shoved his hands in his pockets and walked down the hill.

Emma frowned at Mark's abrupt departure and wondered what she'd said to drive him away.

A year after Meg's death, Mark still couldn't utter the word "widower." The sense of peace he found in the wilderness hadn't ever been interrupted by a pretty woman—until today. He sat on a log, closed his eyes, and breathed as visions of Meg with her long, blond hair and sunny smile popped into his brain. He missed his wedding ring and the comfort it brought him, and he rubbed the finger where it usually lived.

A shadow cast on Mark as Helen stepped in front of him, blocking the sun. "Sorry to interrupt, but the afternoon session starts in a few minutes."

"Okay. Thanks."

The guests gathered by the shore. Emma stood in the circle beside Penny.

"Do you think we can do this?" Penny asked Emma.

"I guess we'll find out."

Jim didn't squander time with instruction. "There are two ways to bring the canoe onto your shoulders," Jim began. "The first way is to stand alongside and grip the gunwales, or canoe sides, with either hand, then hoist it over your head. The second way is for one person to hold the canoe upside down with both hands on the gunwales and the bow on the ground. Your partner scoots under the boat, balances the yoke on their shoulders, and lifts it into the air. Either way works. Choose a comfortable method for your team. Helen, please show the group."

Helen stood beside a canoe, grabbed the gunwales, lifted it straight into the air, and settled it onto her shoulders. She balanced the canoe and walked forward.

"Wow, I'm impressed," said Emma.

Penny nudged Emma and said, under her breath, "She's *strong*."

Helen brought the canoe to the ground. She turned the canoe upside down, lifted it, and walked past the middle. The canoe cleared her head, and she held the sides. Jim ducked under the canoe and settled it on his shoulders.

"Everyone, grab a partner, and let's practice the canoe portage."

The other guests shifted partners, but Emma and Penny stayed together.

"I'm not strong enough to deadlift a canoe. What do you think?" said Penny.

"Agreed," said Emma. "Let's try the second option."

Penny wanted to try the portage first. Together, they turned the canoe upside down. Emma lifted the canoe from the back. She walked her hands past the yoke, held the heavy canoe in place, and called out, "Go for it, Penny!" Penny ducked under the canoe and settled the yoke on her shoulders.

"I've got it," said Penny. Emma let go and scrambled out from under the canoe. Penny walked with the canoe on her shoulders.

"Way to go, Penny. You rock! Is it heavy? Can you see in front of you?"

"It's not terrible, and when I shift the canoe upward, I see the horizon."

Emma stole a glance at Mark, currently carrying his canoe with ease. His blue eyes had lost the sparkle they'd had this morning, and she remembered his abrupt departure from the porch. Distracted, she didn't hear Penny yell, "Emma! Emma, I need help!"

Penny had set the canoe down on its bow, but needed help. "Oops, sorry." Emma said as she raced over, and together they brought the canoe to the ground.

They spent the rest of the afternoon in the lake or on the shore honing their new skills.

"Nice work today, folks," said Jim. "Master the basics for a strong trip. Remember, one of you will always portage the canoe and the other will haul gear. Enjoy your half-hour break, and then we'll meet at the firepits to build a campfire. Your dinner tonight depends upon a successful fire. If you fail, self-serve peanut butter and jelly sandwiches are available in the lodge. We'll see you soon."

Penny ran to the bathhouse while Emma hiked up the hill behind Mark.

"Hey, Mark," Emma called. Mark stopped and turned around and waited for Emma to catch up to him. "Um, I'm sorry about earlier—on the porch. I didn't mean to upset you."

Mark waved his hand. "It's fine. Forget it." They walked toward the open field. "So . . . do you know how to build a fire?"

Emma hung her head. "Peanut butter and jelly are in my future tonight for sure."

Mark laughed and Emma tingled from the deep baritone sound. "The first time I built a fire, I spent half a day trying to get thick pieces of wood to light."

Emma smiled and nodded but didn't have the foggiest idea what he meant.

Penny joined Emma at the firepits, and the group circled Jim as he lectured on practical ways to build a campfire and environmental concerns surrounding fire in dense woods. He instructed them on wood collection and forest-fire prevention. Emma wished she had a notebook to write down all the new information. Camping was a complicated activity.

Penny'd built fires as a kid with her family, so Emma tagged along behind her as they collected tinder, kindling, and larger pieces of firewood in the forest next to the field. They returned with armloads of wood, and Penny taught Emma how to build a pyramid with the tinder. She lit the pyramid and blew on the fire. As flames sparked, Penny sang.

"*It only takes a spark to get a fire going. And soon all those around will warm up to its glowing . . .*"

Emma smiled at her. "Your voice is beautiful."

Penny's neck flushed. "My family sang that song when we built campfires on vacation. Our parents taught us it wouldn't light if you didn't sing."

"I'm so glad you know how to build a fire. Peanut butter and jelly wouldn't fill the hole in my stomach tonight. I need real food," said Emma. Penny added larger pieces of kindling to the fire and flames shot into the air. After the fire burned down, she showed Emma how to place the foil-wrapped meals beneath the embers to cook.

Emma picked at a nail. "Can I tell you something?"

"Sure."

"I don't think I can sleep on the ground for ten nights. And the whole bathroom thing? This is crazy."

"We'll be super tired, so sleeping won't be hard. It's easy to pee in the woods, but a period in the wilderness sucks."

Emma did some mental math and exhaled. "Geez. I didn't factor my period into this mess."

"So, what's your story?"

Emma poked at the fire. "My husband cheated on me, and our divorce was finalized in March. I wanted a break from the city, and I couldn't afford to lose the money when I screwed up the registration. I needed a vacation after a tough school year."

"Wow. I'm sorry. A guy cheated on me in high school. My brothers beat him up. Do you have brothers to beat up your ex?"

Emma laughed. "No. I'm an only child."

"You can borrow my brothers any time."

"Thanks."

Emma and Penny opened their foil packets, and the hot steam escaped into the cool air. Emma took her first bite of the meat, potatoes, and vegetables.

"Hmmm." Emma closed her eyes and savored the meal. "Does all campfire food taste this delicious?"

"I've burned my share of food over an open flame, but if cooked well, it tastes awesome."

They extinguished the fires with buckets of water from the lake, and the sun dipped below the tree line as they cleaned up. The red sky reflected off the lake, and pink, cotton-candy clouds dotted the sky. Jim announced tomorrow's agenda of tents, knots, and first-aid review.

Guests peeled off to their separate cabins. One gentleman

left after dinner, blaming a stomach bug. The lodge vans ran day and night, back and forth to Duluth.

Emma showered with the daddy longlegs and brushed her teeth. Helen joined her in the bathhouse. "How're you?"

"I'm sore from the paddle, but the portage is easy enough," said Emma.

"Portage is easy here on the property, but a canoe on your head through woods is a challenge. Hills, rocks, and over-hanging tree branches create obstacles that can lengthen a portage."

"Oh," said Emma, slumping against the sink counter.

Helen patted her on the arm. "We'll work together. I've canoed hundreds of miles and haven't died yet."

Emma thanked her as they walked back to their cabin. She climbed into her sleeping bag, and the cicadas lulled her to sleep.

Chapter Seven

AT DAWN, rain was pelting the metal roof of the cabin, and Emma expected an altered schedule, but when she got to the lodge for breakfast, Jim insisted the activities would proceed as planned to prepare them for any conditions that might occur on the trip. The group carried tents to the open field and Emma and Penny struggled with the long poles and the fabric of the tent for half an hour in torrential downpour. Eventually, they tossed the wet contraption onto the ground. Emma's hair dripped onto her face, and puddles formed at her feet. The blisters on her ankles persisted, worsening by the hour.

"This sucks," said Penny.

"We need help," said Emma. She stared at the mess on the ground with her hands on her hips and shivered in the cold rain.

Mark jogged over to them. His baseball hat kept his hair and face dry, but his wet T-shirt clung to his body and outlined the muscles in his biceps and pecs. Emma's mouth watered, and she stifled a moan. Mark showed them how to insert the poles into the fabric and, before long, the tent stood tall, so they dashed inside of it to escape the rain. The interior of the tent brought the three of them closer together and muffled the noise of the rain outside.

"Thanks. We never would have figured out the tent without you," said Emma, squeezing the water out of her hair.

"No problem. Camping in the rain is not ideal, but it happens. Our trip is ten days and I'm sure we'll hit all sorts of weather."

Penny rubbed Mark's bicep. "So . . . you're pretty strong for an old man."

Emma slapped a hand to her forehead. "Penny."

"I'm thirty-five but graying early like my dad. I keep in shape by camping and playing hockey. I lift a little weight on the side."

Penny raised one eyebrow and murmured, "More than a little."

Emma cleared her throat. "Our next session is knots. Let's go."

"Sounds good." Mark held the tent door open and offered his hand to Penny and then Emma to help them out of the tent. Emma accepted Mark's hand, and a spark of heat jolted between them. She tilted her face up to Mark's. A bewildered look crossed his face, and they dropped hands and hiked toward the lodge.

Mark begged off to the bathhouse and rested his hands on the sink. The mirror reflected his blank look, so he breathed a long breath and closed his eyes until Meg filled his mind. Her smile settled him and dismissed the flutter in his chest when he'd held Emma's hand.

· · ·

"Why do we need to learn how to tie knots?" Emma asked Jim in the conference room of the lodge.

"We will secure the canoes at night so they don't float away in a storm, and we'll tie our food bags up in the trees to keep bears away."

"Bears?" Emma whispered with wide eyes.

"You betcha," said Jim.

The first-aid refresher proved routine for Emma. She received first-aid and CPR training every fall before school and dealt with broken bones and gashes on the playground. Jim encouraged the group to practice their new skills, so Penny and Emma canoed before lunch. Their rain gear kept their bodies dry, but their hair was plastered to their heads by the time they hiked back to the lodge. Helen sat rocking on the front porch when Emma and Penny arrived.

"Buy a waterproof baseball hat in the lodge gift shop, girls. You'll thank me later," said Helen.

"Thanks," replied Emma.

After they finished their sloppy joes, Penny handed Emma the first-aid kit. Emma winced as she pulled off a hiking boot and a wet wool sock. The popped blister on her right foot bled with each step, enlarging the wound. She used a napkin to blot the blood and attempted to dry the area to receive a bandage.

"Ouch. Let me help you." Mark sat across from her, picked up her right foot, and cradled it in his large, warm hand. He dried the area, applied antiseptic ointment, and gently placed a Band-Aid over the wound. "Your feet are so small," he whispered. He kneaded her foot and set it down on the floor. He picked up her other foot and untied her boot, removed her sock, and repeated his ministrations on her left foot. The intimate touch warmed her from head to toe and her heart tumbled around in her chest.

He cleared his throat. "Wear a dry pair of socks this afternoon. Can Penny go back to the cabin and get some for you?"

She blinked. "Uh, yeah, of course. Thanks."

A fire in the rain proved near impossible, no matter how many times they sang Penny's song, and slippery mud created a dangerous canoe portage. When Emma's paddle got stuck in some lake weeds and almost capsized them, she quit. She stored the canoe, hung her life jacket, and stomped up the hill. She slammed into the cabin and threw her clothes into her bag and backpack. She dumped her gear on the lodge porch and went inside to ask the departure time of the next shuttle.

The pretty girl at the desk smiled and said, "The next shuttle leaves in an hour."

"Great. I'll be on it."

She returned to the porch, collapsed into a rocker, and held her head in her hands.

"Emma?"

Emma swiped tears from her dirt-stained face, and Mark furrowed his brow. "I can't." She shook her head and tears fell onto her lap. "I can't do this," she whimpered.

Mark sat down beside her. "Don't leave."

"I can't build a fire, pitch a tent, or tie a knot. I'm wet and cold and my ankles are killing me. We haven't even started the trip and my cute clothes are dirty. Who am I kidding? I've never camped a day in my life."

Mark smiled. "The weather sucks today, and lousy weather can ruin a fun time in the wilderness. But I want you to stay. You're awesome. You've learned how to steer and portage the canoe, and you're the best at first aid. We'll work together on the trip, and I think we'll have a memorable experience."

"I don't think I can," she whispered.

"It's your decision, of course, but either way, I'm glad we met."

Emma grinned at Mark through her tears and sighed. He squeezed her shoulder and went inside the lodge.

The internal debate of whether to leave or stay warred in Emma's head for the next hour. Physical exhaustion overwhelmed every fiber of her being, and ten days of this work might kill her. The lack of bathrooms in the wilderness turned her stomach. She struggled to sleep on the bunk in the cabin, and the ground would be worse. But the scenery and the quiet of the wilderness entranced her. She liked her new friends, and honestly, she didn't want another failure in her life.

Chapter Eight

THE LODGE VAN LOADED UP, but Emma waved goodbye to it and brought her gear back to the cabin to stay another day. She stood in the shower until the hot water ran out and slipped on dry leggings and a long-sleeved T-shirt. Flip-flops gave her ankles a break, and a warm, chicken pot pie dinner turned her mood around. Mark changed the bandages on her feet after dinner, and the guests, now six, relaxed by the fireplace. Tom and Bob, brothers from Wisconsin, were lifelong canoe campers. They both had bald heads and square frames and wore flannel shirts in a variety of colors. Veterans of Northern Woods trips, they passed the time with cards and cribbage. Their team consisted of three women and three men. Jim prepared to guide from a solo canoe.

The group talked for a while, and then Emma yawned and said, "I'm beat. I think I'll head back to the cabin. Good night, everyone."

"Hold on, I'll walk with you," said Mark.

. . .

They walked toward the cabins in the moonlight.

Mark held onto her elbow as they navigated the thin path to the cabins. She leaned into him as they walked, and an electrical charge arced between them.

"I'm glad you stayed."

They stood beside the cabins and regarded each other. Emma shifted from foot to foot and slapped a mosquito on her arm. "Thanks. I couldn't stomach another failure in my life. My divorce is still fresh, and I'm here to figure out my next steps."

"I'm sorry about your divorce," said Mark.

"Thanks." She mumbled and disappeared into the women's cabin.

Mark tossed and turned in his sleeping bag in the men's cabin. Moonlight filtered through the small cabin window, and visions of Emma mixed with memories of Meg and kept him awake.

The smells of frying bacon and hot coffee lured the team out of their bunks and to the lodge early the next morning. All six team members shared a round table in the dining room and Emma devoured sweet French toast and sipped her tea while she talked with Bob and Helen. As soon as she'd started to relax, Jim addressed the team.

"Good morning. I trust you all slept well. Today, we will begin with team-building activities, then compass and map skills. After lunch, we will pack our gear for the 'put in' tomorrow morning. Let's go!"

Emma shivered in the open field used for team building and pulled her heavy sweatshirt over her T-shirt. She rubbed her arms to stay warm and ran back to the cabin for pants. The first two activities mimicked easy ones she'd participated in as a teacher at staff development sessions. She even took charge of the human knot challenge.

"The final team challenge today will be a trust fall," said Jim. He led them over to a picnic table and told the team to form two rows. "One team member will stand backward on the picnic table edge, cross their arms over their chest, and fall backward into the arms of their teammates."

Penny climbed onto the picnic table first. Jim positioned himself at the top of the group to protect her head. They lined up in two rows, and Emma sweated and waited for her turn.

Penny turned around with her arms crossed over her chest, closed her eyes, and said, "Ready?" The team answered, "Yes, go!" Penny fell back, and they caught her, no problem. She jumped up and grinned. She moved into one of the rows, and Mark climbed onto the table. Mark fell without issue, despite his six-foot-two height. Tom and Helen fell off the table next. Emma's stomach twisted tighter with each fall. Bob, the heaviest of the group, completed his fall.

"Emma. Your turn," said Jim.

She climbed onto the picnic table, testing its stability with each foot as she stepped. Once atop the table, she shuffled to the edge, turned backward, crossed arms over her chest, and then turned around to examine the group.

"C'mon, you can do it!" said Penny.

"You're the smallest of all of us. We've got you," said Tom.

She turned back around and counted to three, but her feet remained stuck to the picnic table. She wiped her sweaty hands on her pants, inhaled through her nose, and reset. The team encouraged her, but their voices sounded muffled in her panicky state.

"You can do this!" said Mark. "We're here for you. We'll catch you. Trust us."

Emma listened to his words, closed her eyes, said a small prayer, and fell back. Hands and bodies closed around her. When she opened her eyes, Mark's blue eyes locked with hers. He smiled and shouted, "Way to go!"

Emma's heart flip-flopped, and she said thanks and joined her team on the ground.

"Let's return to the lodge to interpret maps and pack," said Jim.

The group gathered in the conference room, and Jim passed out laminated trip maps. He lectured on compass and map skills in the event someone got separated or lost. Emma feigned interest and braided her hair while Jim droned. She spent the session on basic orienteering daydreaming about how Mark's hands held her ankles when he bandaged them. She caught the part of the presentation about the emergency satellite phone the guide carried, and Jim finally dismissed them for lunch. Emma, first in line for the grilled paninis and homemade mac and cheese at the buffet station, loaded her plate.

She talked with Bob about his granddaughter's college program in education while Mark and Helen discussed local politics and Penny pummeled Jim with questions about bear, moose, and other potential animal sightings. Emma bussed her dishes and headed out to the porch. After a while, the lodge's door opened.

"Hey, it's time to pack the gear. Are you all right?" asked Mark.

"There's so much to remember. This reminds me of the night before I left for college. I'm prepared, but uncertain about what lies ahead."

"Understood. This is a challenging trip for a rookie camper, but you can do it."

Penny peeked out of the door. "Hey guys, it's time to pack. Come on in."

Tables lined with camping gear filled the lodge's conference room.

Jim addressed the group. "We'll pass out gear and instruct on each piece, then you'll return to your cabins to pack. The lodge will store your extra luggage in this conference room. Northern Woods will welcome new guests to the cabins the day after tomorrow."

Back in their cabin, Penny and Emma dumped the gear collected in the lodge onto empty bunks and listened as Helen advised them how to pack.

"Pack as light as possible. Remember, you can turn underwear inside out. Pack a warm sweatshirt, rain gear, plenty of warm socks, a swimsuit, and a variety of shorts, pants, and T-shirts. Prepare for all kinds of weather: wind, rain, cold, heat, and humidity. No one cares how you look or smell."

"Ew. I hate it when I smell," said Emma.

"Sleep in a T-shirt, and keep the bags light. Remember, what you pack, you haul. We split communal gear like tents, cookware, food, and common supplies between canoes."

Emma and Penny exchanged worried looks.

"It's normal to feel overwhelmed. The food pack will lighten as we eat, but we'll collect and haul our garbage," said Helen.

"What do we eat on the trail?" asked Penny.

"The lodge packs freeze-dried food, noodles, oatmeal, peanut butter sandwiches, and granola," said Helen. "If we arrive at our campsite early enough, we fish. Fresh fish cooked over an open flame is a special treat in the wilderness."

"Do we wash the dishes in the lake?" asked Emma.

"No. We haul buckets of water two hundred feet away from the lakes and do dishes in the woods. We'll show you how when we get there."

"Is the lake water safe to drink?" asked Penny.

"We filter or boil any water used to drink, cook, or wash dishes," answered Helen. "If you get ill from unfiltered water, it's miserable. Jim is a pro and will help us."

"I'm done. I need a shower," said Penny.

"Same," said Emma.

Penny and Emma headed to the bathhouse while Helen packed. Emma stood under the warm shower and scrubbed her body. She lingered over her breasts, remembering Mark's smile after her trust fall. His strong arms caught her around her shoulders and his plump lips framed his wide smile. The pull toward him increased in intensity with every interaction. Her nipples pebbled in her hands and warmth spread through her body. She toyed with her breasts and fantasized about Mark's large hands cupped under them and his wet lips wrapped around the hard nub.

"Did you shave your legs?" Penny called.

Emma snapped back to reality. "Yeah—be out in a minute." Oh well. Fantasies about a hot guy in a shower in the middle of nowhere never hurt anyone. Besides, the daddy longlegs wouldn't tell.

The steady stream of cool water over Mark's head slowed his heart rate and loosened the tension he held in his muscles over his physical attraction to Emma. Her round eyes, the color of chocolate syrup, intrigued him; and his hands itched to remove the band from her ponytail and run his fingers through her brown waves. Her lean figure and gutsy personality fueled his desire. He scrubbed himself under the cool water to wash away his lust for the small woman from Chicago.

After he'd dried off and dressed in shorts and a T-shirt in the cabin, he spied her walking the path to the lodge with Penny. Her ponytail bounced and her wide smile twisted his heart. He didn't have time for another cold shower, so he trekked to the lodge for dinner.

The lodge's dining staff had filled the buffet with a full roast beef dinner, complete with a trifle for dessert. Mark was loading his plate when a clatter sounded and a fork skidded across the slippery floor and hit his shoe. He picked it up and looked around. Emma, dressed in a light pink sweatshirt and navy shorts, blushed when he caught her eye. He tossed her utensil into the wash bucket and grabbed a new one. He walked over to her. "I think you need a new fork," said Mark.

"Yeah."

Mark handed her the fork and their fingers brushed against each other's.

"Thanks."

"Any time."

After dinner, Helen asked Mark to go for a walk.

"Sure," said Mark.

They started down the hill. "I like to get to know my canoe partner before the trip. It helps with communication."

"Smart."

"My husband passed away twelve years ago. We canoed the Boundary Waters together every summer, but when he died, I didn't want to travel solo, so I booked a Northern Woods trip and loved it. I've returned every summer."

"You're a widow? I'm sorry for your loss."

"Thanks. Some days are easier than others even twelve years later."

"Hmph," said Mark.

"Mark?" Helen stopped and touched his elbow.

Mark stopped and took a deep breath. "My wife, Meg, died a year ago last April."

"Oh, my dear. You're young to be a widower."

"Camping and being in the wilderness heals my soul enough to live through the days. I came to Northern Woods to learn how to navigate the lakes. I never imagined my canoe partner would be a widow, too."

"We'll make a great team." She patted his arm.

They finished their walk, and Mark joined Emma as she rocked on the porch. The orange sun made its final descent behind the trees and cast shadows on the property while fireflies blinked in the darkness. The rocker creaked under Emma. He sat in the rocker beside her and added to the noise. They rocked without words until Mark said, "Your spot-on directions helped the team with the human knot challenge."

"I teach first grade and give directions for a living."

"You're a teacher?" asked Mark. "You must love kids."

"I love their wide-eyed wonderment and their eagerness to absorb whatever you teach them. They're sponges in elementary school. Are you a father?"

Mark cleared his throat. "No."

Meg had visited her ob-gyn in July. "We stopped birth

control three months ago," Meg said. "I'm done with coffee and alcohol. We eat organic vegetables, and Mark wears boxer shorts. I've tracked my temperature and taken ovulation tests. We've tried for a month."

Her doctor nodded and examined her breasts. She applied pressure to the right breast and palpated the tissue. She scowled and said, "Meg, does it hurt when I press on your armpit here?"

"No," answered Meg.

"Meg, there is a lump in your right breast. Let's do a mammogram to be safe."

"I'm twenty-eight. I need a mammogram?"

"Yes. Are you free tomorrow?"

"Sure. I guess," Meg answered.

The first mammogram led to a series of detailed mammograms and a breast ultrasound. The ultrasound showed a large lump in Meg's right breast. The doctor biopsied the lump. The doctors reassured them, saying that benign cysts developed with birth control and to relax and wait for pathology. The pathology came back a week later, and their lives changed forever.

"What about you? Do you and your ex-husband have kids?"

"I wanted children, but I'm grateful I didn't drag any through the divorce."

Mark asked her more questions about her career, and she told funny stories about the kids she'd taught for the next hour. She tucked her legs under her, and the moonlight bathed her face in a soft glow. Her laughter filled the night air while she animatedly told stories.

An owl hooted in the forest and its call bounced off the side of the lodge. Emma was startled by the strange sound. "Tomorrow is an early morning. I need to sleep," said Emma.

"Good idea," answered Mark. They stepped off the porch and descended the hill, careful to avoid the rocks on the path.

"Don't let those loons keep you awake tonight." Mark winked. "You'll need every ounce of energy tomorrow."

"For sure." She nudged him as they neared the cabins. The invisible spark flashed between them, and Emma sidestepped to her cabin.

"Good night," he whispered.

Chapter Nine

MILK COVERED the cereal in the bowl and drowned the flakes. Emma poked at it for a few minutes, but her stomach roiled the morning of the 'put-in.' She tossed her spoon into the soggy mess as bile rose in her throat. She stood, her chair crashed to the ground, and she ran for the door. She scampered down the steps and ran around the side of the building. Large hands pulled her hair back from her face as she threw up on a patch of wildflowers.

"Take your time," Mark said from behind her. He rubbed small circles on her back and waited until she finished. Emma stood and wiped her mouth.

"Sorry, I lose it when I'm nervous."

"Don't apologize. Remember, we're all in this together. We'll help one another."

Mark let go of her hair but kept his hand on her back. Emma gathered her hair into a ponytail.

"Can I get you anything?" asked Mark.

"A dry piece of toast would be great. I don't want to start the day on an empty stomach, but if I look at cereal again . . ."

"I'll be right back. Wait on the porch."

Emma sat on the porch steps and took deep breaths in through her nose and out of her mouth. A few minutes later, the door opened and Mark returned with a piece of dry toast.

"Thanks." Emma nibbled a corner and waited to see if her stomach would tolerate it. She took a bigger bite. The lodge door opened again, and Penny stepped outside.

"Hey Emma, whatcha doin' blowing chunks? You're not trying to ditch me, are you?"

Emma grinned. "No, of course not. Just nervous."

"Well, it looks like you're in capable hands." Penny winked and giggled. She grabbed her gear and ran down the hill, her red curly hair bouncing on her back.

"I bet she kept her parents on edge in high school," said Mark.

Emma smirked. "I'm sure her three older brothers kept her in line."

"I need to grab my gear. Are you all right?" asked Mark.

"I'll be fine. Thanks."

Mark smiled and squeezed her hand.

Emma hauled her gear down the hill and joined Penny at the lakeshore. Canoes and paddles lined the beach, and the communal gear rested nearby. Emma and Penny volunteered to haul the women's tent along with their personal dry packs. The rest of the group approached the area, and they divided the rest of the gear up. Helen and Mark hauled the food and cookware, Bob and Tom loaded the men's tent and the fishing gear. Jim carried the tools. The lodge had outfitted the canoes with yoke pads to soften the weight on their shoulders.

Jim snapped a picture of the group with a disposable camera, and then pairs loaded their canoes and pushed into the lake. The lodge staff whooped and hollered from the front porch, waved goodbye, and shouted, "Good luck!"

Penny paddled from the bow while Emma steered from the stern. Emma's stomach clenched when she glanced back at the lodge, with its hot food and indoor plumbing. But when she turned back to the lake, her heart soared at the beauty of the open-water paddle. The still water reflected the colorful canoes like a piece of art and the wall of green framed the picture. Sun warmed the cool morning air and Emma kept a watchful eye on the sky.

Once they established a rhythm, Jim explained the plan to canoe five miles and complete one portage for an easy first day. He said the map showed the half-mile portage covered flat terrain. Emma relaxed when she learned of the easy portage and didn't focus on filtered water and food cooked over an open flame.

Their practice paid off, and they kept up with the other teams. An hour into the paddle, Penny whipped around in the canoe and pointed her paddle toward the red canoe. "Check him out," she giggled.

Emma followed her gaze and, sure enough, Mark had removed his T-shirt, and with every pull of the paddle, his back muscles flexed. Emma enjoyed the show until Penny yelled at her to straighten out their boat.

The group muted conversation to spot wildlife, and they stopped at an empty campsite for lunch. Emma stretched out on a sunny rock after lunch, and Mark sat down beside her.

"How're you holding up?"

"My ankles or my stomach?"

Mark smiled. "Both."

"Better." She sat up on her elbows. "Aren't you worried about the sun on your back when you take your shirt off in the canoe?"

"I slathered on sunscreen before we left but need to reapply it. Can you help me with my back?"

Emma swallowed hard and squeaked out, "Sure."

Mark returned with the sunscreen from his pack and squeezed some onto her palm. She rubbed it into Mark's expansive back. She started at the top of his shorts and worked up to his broad shoulders. She let her fingers linger on his shoulders long after the lotion dissolved into his skin.

Mark spread the lotion on his chest and arms. "Well, let's get packed up for the rest of the trip today. Our first campsite awaits us."

Emma rubbed her warm hands together and frowned when Mark slipped his T-shirt back on and repacked his lotion.

Packs and canoes littered the portage entrance. Emma wiped the sweat off her face with the hem of her T-shirt. She retied her ponytail and gulped down water. "Nice work, folks," said Jim. "Remember to stay hydrated." Jim led the group through the portage. He wore a pack and carried his solo canoe. The teams hoisted their canoes and hiked through the woods. Emma helped Penny get situated before she started the portage. She wore one pack and carried the tent in her arms. The gear left at the portage entrance would require a second trip by a few team members. Helen brought up the rear.

Emma navigated around branches, rocks, and downed tree limbs. The tree canopy provided shade and kept the group cool on the hike. Wildflowers and the dreaded poison ivy littered the trail. At one point, she slipped and stumbled on a moss-covered rock and had to grab a tree branch to steady herself.

"Are you all right?" asked Helen.

"Yep, thanks. The portage is tough."

"It can be downright dangerous in the woods. Slow and steady."

Emma glimpsed the break in the tree canopy which signaled the end of the trail. She dropped her pack when she got there, and helped Penny lower the canoe to the ground.

"Whew," said Penny. "We survived our first portage." Penny and Emma high-fived. A new lake glistened in the sun and the group rested. Emma lay back against a tree and bathed in the triumph over her first portage while Tom and Mark returned with the rest of the gear.

"Let's go," said Jim. "The setup of camp is the hardest part of the first night." The group loaded into the canoes and onto the new lake.

Emma pointed. "What are those birds?"

"Loons," said Penny.

"The birds from the other night?"

"Yup."

"Loons eat a ton of fish," said Bob.

"They're like an airplane and need a long runway to take flight," said Helen.

"Their calls are sorrowful if they separate from their mate," said Mark. "It's the saddest sound in the world."

The teams exited and unloaded the canoes on the small beach. Emma waited in the boat and stretched her neck to catch a glimpse of the campsite. She saw a firepit and a flat area for tents. Jim instructed the group to split into smaller groups to set up camp. Bob and Tom left to gather firewood while the rest of the group carried the packs and gear to the clearing. The brothers returned with armloads of wood, arguing.

"I'm tellin' you, that bird was an osprey," said Bob.

"No. It was a sharp-shinned hawk," said Tom.

Bob scoffed. "You're wrong. I could see it was an osprey from a mile away."

"You need your eyes checked."

"Problem, gentlemen?" asked Jim.

"No. Bob's wrong again," said Tom.

"Quit your bickering and dump the wood so I can build the fire," said Emma.

Mark chuckled at her comment. "Your teacher's tone will come in handy on this trip."

"I suppose."

After Emma lit the fire, she helped Penny and Helen pitch the women's tent while Mark and Tom handled the men's. Jim secured the knots to tie the food bag, and Bob prepped dinner.

Dinner cooked over the campfire, Jim and Bob studied the maps, and Emma strolled to the lakeshore, ignoring the growl in her stomach. Mark sat on a rock facing the expansive lake.

"Hey," said Emma.

"How's your stomach?" asked Mark.

"Better than my arms and shoulders. My muscles will scream tomorrow."

"I'll work out your kinks with a shoulder rub tonight."

"Um, sure. After dinner around the campfire?"

"It's a date."

"Dinner!" Bob called from the firepit.

"Thank God, I'm starving," said Mark.

The teams devoured a bland, freeze-dried meal of meat products, veggies, and rice with bread on the side. Jim filtered lake water and mixed it with a lemonade packet, and the sweet taste livened the group. After the meal, Helen and Bob hauled the water to do the dishes, and Penny and Mark washed them in the woods under Jim's direction.

The group sat around the campfire while Bob and Tom played cribbage and bickered over the score. Emma placed herself on the ground in front of Mark and melted under the weight of his large hands kneading her shoulders and arms. His palms rubbed circles on her upper back, and she bowed her head to hide the flush on her cheeks from the group. When his hands engulfed her shoulders, Emma squeezed her thighs together to relieve the pleasurable throb. Her breasts pressed against her shirt, and she stifled a whimper when Mark's fingers trailed up her neck and under her hair. One by one, the campers retreated to the tents when darkness engulfed the site. Mark pulled his hands from her shoulders.

"Thanks."

Mark and Emma extinguished the fire and lingered beside the tents.

"Get some good sleep," said Mark.

"Night," said Emma.

Emma changed out of her dirty clothes and settled into her sleeping bag. Penny slithered around to face her and whispered, "I think Mark likes you."

She flipped onto her back and said, "Don't be silly. Besides, it doesn't matter. Focus on the trip."

"Yep. For sure. It's super fun to watch the tension between you two."

Emma rolled her eyes. She settled into her sleeping bag and maneuvered her body around rocks and roots to seek comfort on the unfamiliar surface.

Chapter Ten

An itch on her stomach woke Emma at dawn. She lay in her bag and scratched around her waist until it drove her out of her sleeping bag. She lifted her T-shirt. Tons of red dots covered her bikini line. She pulled on a pair of shorts and sat on a log by the firepit, itching until Mark and Bob emerged from the tent.

Mark rubbed his eyes. "Emma?"

"Red, itchy dots all over my stomach. Help me. What is it?"

"I need the woods," said Bob.

"Let me see," said Mark. Emma lifted her shirt and pulled down her shorts. Mark bent his head to inspect her stomach. "Oh, you've got chigger bites."

"Chiggers?" Emma's shorts snapped back into place.

"Tiny bugs who hang out in tight spaces and feed on your skin cells. Some women sleep in loose boxer shorts when they camp. Do you have any?"

"No. What can I do? They itch."

"Calamine lotion will ease the itch. You'll be fine. Try not to scratch."

Emma pulled on a sweatshirt and stomped into the woods.

When she returned to the campsite, Jim handed her the first-aid kit, and she slathered the lotion on her stomach.

Mark called to her. "Emma, here you go." He tossed her a pair of clean boxer shorts.

"Thanks." She stuffed them into her pack.

Helen cooked over an open flame, preparing a delicious oatmeal breakfast. After breakfast, the teams broke camp. Helen, Bob, and Tom collapsed tents, untied the food bags, and packed their dry packs with ease. Emma grimaced and scratched her bites with every push and pull as she tried to maneuver her sleeping bag into her pack.

"Let me help you," Mark said. He grabbed Emma's sleeping bag and stuffed it into the pack. "Try not to scratch. You don't want an infection."

Emma scowled. "I can't. It's awful."

"My first case of chiggers in the wilderness sucked. I get it. Apply the lotion and you'll curb the itchiness."

The teams pushed through the tough day. Penny struggled up a steep hill with the canoe on her shoulders on the afternoon portage. "Are you all right?" Emma asked her partner.

"I need a break," said Penny.

Emma jogged up to her and helped her set the canoe on the ground. Emma worked her hair up into a ponytail under her hat and welcomed the cool breeze on her neck. Penny swiped her face with her T-shirt and ended up with a streak of mud across her cheek. They both nursed blisters on their palms from the paddles and blew on their hands to cool the burn. They sank to the ground for a break, leaning against trees.

"This is super hard," said Penny.

"And we're young and in shape," said Emma.

"How do Helen, Bob, and Tom make this look so easy?" asked Penny.

"We're seasoned pros," said Helen as she approached the women, carrying a heavy pack. "Wilderness skills use different muscle groups and a different stamina than a run on a treadmill," said Helen. "Your body will adjust over time."

"I'll portage the canoe. You grab the gear," said Emma.

The exhausted team breathed a sigh of relief when the campsite came into view later in the afternoon. Emma spotted a cluster of large rocks in the lake. The water sloshed across them and created bubbles.

"A natural jacuzzi," said Helen. "Grab a swimsuit. I promise, your muscles will thank you."

The group raced to complete the tasks to set up camp and changed into bathing suits. Mark beat the everyone to the shore, tossed his T-shirt onto the ground, and waded to the boulders.

"Be careful, the rocks are slippery." Mark settled on a large rock and water rushed over his body. "This is awesome. Come on in!"

Mark splayed out on the boulder, revealing his chiseled abs and well-defined biceps. The hair on his chest glistened in the sun and Emma's eyes followed a trail of hair down to the waistband of his board shorts. Her nipples tightened under her black one piece as she gawked at Mark and navigated the slick rocks.

"The lake is ice," said Emma.

"It's June," said Helen. "The water won't be warmer until August."

Emma, determined to soothe her muscles, eased onto the rock. The water kneaded her back and calmed the chigger bites. She shivered but stretched her legs and angled her face to the sun. Penny slipped her curly hair into a topknot and joined her.

"Ahh," murmured Penny.

Jim caught the image of the group in the water on camera and took a few shots of the spectacular views. The group relaxed on the rocks and chatted in the late afternoon sun. Dinner and chores followed.

Later, Mark lay on his back in his sleeping bag with his arms over his head and his eyes closed, unable to sleep. Bob's snores drowned out the cicadas and his thoughts strayed to Emma. The natural surroundings entranced her, and she tackled new experiences with grit. She pushed herself to keep up with the group in the canoe and on the portages. After he replayed the past few days with Emma and envisioned her sweet figure in her black swimsuit, he flopped onto his stomach and nudged Bob to stop his snores.

Chapter Eleven

THE SUN BEAT down on the campers as they canoed toward their campsite on day three of their trip. The trees in the forest stood still, and even the birds ceased their chatter.

"If we arrive early to our site, we should fish," said Mark.

"A fat walleye would taste better than the freeze-dried gruel we've eaten," said Tom.

"The fish ain't gonna bite in this heat," said Bob, shaking his head.

"Can't hurt to try. Fish will be a tasty change of pace," said Tom.

"You'll be wastin' your time," said Bob.

"Oh, for heaven's sake, stop arguing," said Helen. "Mark, pick up the pace. These two sound like my kids when they were toddlers."

Mark and Helen paddled ahead of the group while Bob and Tom mumbled to themselves about fishing.

"Don't scratch," said Penny to Emma. "You'll get an infection."

Emma stopped and leaned forward on her paddle. "I can't help it. It's awful."

"Let's stop for a minute and reapply your lotion," said Penny. "I bet the lotion you applied this morning is mixed with sweat."

"You're probably right." She set her paddle in the canoe and Penny also stopped. Emma fished the lotion out of her pack and slathered it all over her lower stomach and back. "Ahh. Better."

"Great. Let's catch up. The group is up ahead, and we can't lose them."

Their canoe drifted toward the shore when they stopped the paddle, and as Emma slid the lotion back into her pack, she sensed something staring at her. She whipped her head around. "Oh!" Emma clapped her hand over her mouth.

Penny whirled around. "What is it?"

"Look," Emma whispered, "to your right. In the woods. I think it's a moose."

"Where?" Penny whispered.

"Ten feet back from shore. He's staring at me with huge eyes."

"I see him now," said Penny. "He's ginormous!"

He blended in with the trees and bushes near the shore.

Jim paddled back to them. "Are you all right?"

"Shh," whispered Penny. She pointed at the moose.

"I'll go tell everyone else." Jim paddled away to alert the group.

The massive animal ambled near the shore and bent his neck up to eat leaves off a tree. The group approached the scene in silence. Helen nodded and smiled at Penny and Mark whistled low. The moose stuck his long nose out, ate another leaf, and stepped off the shore to drink from the lake. Jim took pictures while the moose waded farther into the lake to cool off, and Emma leaned forward, her forearms on her knees. Her palms sweat and her heart pounded as the wild animal moved close enough to touch in the shallows of the lake. She expected him to topple due to the massive weight of his antlers, but the majestic moose snorted, turned, and retreated into the forest.

"Super cool, but kinda ugly," said Penny.

Bob said, "I can relate. My nose is growin' huge in my old age, too."

Everyone laughed and picked up their paddles to complete the afternoon route.

Once at the campsite, Bob and Tom organized the fishing gear and left to find a shady cove. They placed bets on if the fish would bite or not.

Emma and Penny pitched the women's tent. "I've never fished before, have you?" asked Emma.

"My dad and brothers fished on our camping trips. I'll fish, but I won't clean them. Heads and guts all over the rocks. Yuck. I'll wait for someone to work their magic over the campfire."

"I don't think I need to see the guts," answered Emma. "Why don't we swim instead? It's hot."

"Helen!" Penny called.

"What?" answered Helen as she built a tower of kindling in the campfire pit.

"Join us for a swim?"

"Sure. I'll get my suit on as soon as I finish the fire."

The three women sauntered to the shore in their suits.

"Hey Jim, we're hittin' the lake," said Penny.

"Got it, thanks," answered Jim.

"Have a good swim," said Mark as he readied a canoe to join the anglers.

"Yep," said Penny.

Mark stepped into the canoe and waved.

The trio of women eased into the cool water from a flat rock near the shore. They toed along the rocky bottom to an area large enough to float.

"Ooh . . ." breathed Emma. "The chigger bites don't itch in the water."

Helen floated on her back. "Heaven."

Penny said, "I think the guys can handle the fishing. Besides, I don't think I can spend another minute in a canoe today."

"Agreed," said Emma, floating in the cool water. The quiet lap of the water against the shore and the slight breeze through the trees slowed her breath. The blue sky, devoid of clouds, was the color of a robin's egg and twittering birds provided background music to their lazy afternoon.

"So, what do you think of the trip so far?" asked Helen.

"It's tough, but the scenery is worth the effort," said Emma. "I love the quiet. I've lived in a city or suburb for thirty years and didn't realize the constant noise until it disappeared."

"It's cool, and it's fun to watch Mark fall all over himself around Emma," giggled Penny. "Hey girls, are we alone?"

Emma and Helen twisted their heads around.

"Yeah," said Emma. "Why?"

"I'm gonna ditch my swimsuit. I love skinny-dipping."

"Go for it," said Emma.

Penny whipped off her bikini top and shimmied out of her bottoms. She tossed them on a rock and dove under the water.

"I'll join you," said Helen as she slipped off her tankini top.

Emma peered around again. "Why not?" She stripped off her black one-piece suit and hung it on a tree branch near the shore. She dipped her hair in the lake and her body under the water. "We should listen for the fishermen. We don't want to give Bob or Tom a heart attack."

They swam and gossiped while they floated. The cool water sluiced over Emma's skin and the sensual feeling led her to daydream about Mark splayed on the flat rocks in the lake the previous day.

"Hey, I need to work on my tan. You cool?" asked Penny.

"Sure," said Emma.

Penny climbed onto the flat rock, stretched out, and sighed.

"Oh, to be young and perky," sighed Helen.

Emma chuckled. She swam laps in the cove and spotted small fish and rocks in the crystal-clear lake.

After a while, Tom's voice echoed over the lake. "Girls? Where are you?"

Penny yelped and jumped into the water. They grabbed their suits and held them in front of themselves to cover the important parts before the men rounded the corner. Helen ducked behind a low tree branch near the shore.

"Ladies, check this out," said Tom. "We caught four large . . . oops. Sorry to interrupt."

Mark caught Emma's eye and he opened his mouth to speak but reddened and turned to dock his canoe on shore. The men hurried out of their canoes and carried their gear and the fish up to the campsite.

Mark readied the skillet over the open flame while Bob cleaned the fish with speed and precision, and Tom gathered the guts to burn after dinner. Mark kept his head down and listened as Emma laughed with the women in the tent. They emerged and he avoided her eyes, but her wet suit taunted him from a tree branch.

He grilled the fish and attempted a conversation with Tom about different lures used in the lakes. But he kept stealing glances at Emma, so Tom winked at Mark and patted his shoulder. "Let's talk another time."

After dinner, Mark poked the fire with a stick. Conversation drifted around him.

"Mark? Hey, Mark? Did you hear me?" asked Helen.

"What? Oh sure, I'll wash the dishes in the morning."

The group erupted in laughter. "I asked how you celebrate the Fourth of July, since we're here this year for the holiday," said Helen.

Mark blushed. "Sorry, I zoned out. We used to barbecue with our friends and watch the fireworks at a park near our house."

"I don't care about the Fourth of July, but I would never miss Halloween," said Penny. "Halloween is lit."

"Lit?" asked Bob. "You mean like a lamp?"

Penny tossed her red hair and hooted. "No, like 'awesome.'"

Bob shook his head. "I can't ever understand you young people."

"Halloween *sucks*," growled Emma.

Mark furrowed his brow at Emma but didn't say anything.

Conversation drifted from topic to topic until the campers retreated to the tents.

"I'll douse the campfire," said Emma.

"I'll help you," said Mark.

Mark and Emma grabbed pots to fill with lake water.

"Hey, we didn't mean to embarrass you guys earlier," said Emma as she poured her bucket over the fire, eliciting a hiss.

Mark flushed. "No worries. Glad you had fun."

"It was liberating. The Boundary Waters pushes me out of my comfort zone in a ton of ways."

Mark doused the remainder of the flames with his pot.

They sat close together on a log until the flames fizzled in the fire. Their legs touched, but neither one of them moved.

"Why do you hate Halloween?"

Emma sighed. "I found my husband bangin' his assistant in my shower last Halloween."

Mark's pulse raced and he clenched his hands together. What idiot would cheat on Emma? "I'm so sorry."

"Yeah." Emma shivered in the cool air and pressed her leg tighter to Mark's. His pulse raced even more at the increased pressure and the silkiness of her thigh.

Smoke from the fire trailed up into the air and dissipated. "So, what did you mean when you said 'we' used to barbecue on the Fourth of July?"

Grief slammed into him like a Mack truck. "We'd invite friends over for barbecued ribs and games in the yard. After dark, we'd roast marshmallows in the bonfire while fireworks lit the sky."

"Sounds like fun."

"It was until . . ."

"Until what?"

Mark faced her in the moonlight. Her chocolate-brown eyes pleaded for an explanation, but he said, "Nothing. It's not important."

"The fire is out. I'm exhausted," said Emma. She stood and patted his shoulder.

"Yep. G'night." Mark sat by the extinguished fire long after her tent zipped closed.

The chilly wind blew Emma's ponytail as she sat by the lake after breakfast. Clouds dotted the sky, and the stiff breeze cooled the tea in her hand. Penny burned the reconstituted eggs, but no one complained. The smell of coffee alerted her to a visitor.

"Good morning," said Helen. "How's the itch?"

"Better today."

"You talked with Mark again last night."

"I can't figure him out. He avoids personal questions but is kind and helpful. My chronic habit of falling for attractive men never ends well."

"Well, Mark does belong on some sort of calendar, but doesn't seem like the type to jerk a woman around. We've got a tough day ahead. Focus."

"For sure."

Her swimsuit and shammy dried overnight, and she stuffed them back into her pack. Emma dressed in hiking pants and wore a sweatshirt over her T-shirt. The last of the chigger bites faded on her stomach, and the itch had disappeared overnight. She helped collapse the tent and load gear into the canoes for another day in the Boundary Waters. Emma carried the canoe on the portage and Penny accepted the gear. The sky turned gunmetal gray, and the wind picked up in the afternoon. Emma overcorrected the canoe several times as wind battered their boat. Yesterday's clear blue lake turned gray, and white caps splashed cold water into the boats.

"We've got four miles to go," yelled Jim. "Pick up the pace. A storm is on the horizon."

Emma yanked her hat down farther on her head and worked. Yesterday, she'd skinny-dipped in the calm lake, but today, it churned scary waves.

The group reached their site in the late afternoon, exhausted after the tough paddle. Jim instructed them to forgo a fire, as he predicted the storm would be upon them soon. The tents took four people to pitch, as the wind hindered their efforts. Jim, Tom, and Mark secured both ends of the canoes to trees with the extra rope. No one wanted to lose a canoe. Emma prepared a cold dinner of peanut butter sandwiches and lemonade. The group ate before the rain started, and by dusk, a tremendous light show lit up the western sky.

Emma wrapped her arms around herself against the chill. "It's beautiful."

"The lightning hints at a powerful storm. Helen, are the tents secure?" asked Jim.

"You betcha."

"Stay in your tents. If you need to use the woods, bring a flashlight and a buddy to the forest. Rain and windstorms can disorient you, and we don't need anyone getting lost," said Jim.

The rain started as a drizzle, and everyone retired to the tents. Penny said to Emma, "Let's use the woods before the storm gets crazy."

"Good idea. Grab a flashlight."

The girls unzipped the tent and scampered into the forest.

"It's pitch dark," said Penny.

"Crazy. I can't see my feet in front of me. Let's be quick," responded Emma.

On the way back to the campsite, Emma jumped over a log and slipped in the mud. Her foot caught under a root, and she tumbled backward into a mud puddle. "Agh! Penny, help me!" Emma bellowed. Penny ran back to Emma. She pulled on the root, but Emma's foot wouldn't budge. The sky opened and the heavens released their fury. Rain fell in sheets and wind whistled through the forest.

"Ugh. I can't get your foot out from under this root. Hold on, and I'll grab someone to help us."

She jogged back down the trail to the campsite. Emma sat in the mud and rolled her eyes at her predicament. Every time she yanked her foot, she drove it farther into the mud hole.

Rain and wind pummeled the forest. Penny ran toward her with Mark in tow.

Mark squatted down next to Emma. "Are you hurt?"

"I don't think so. Just stuck."

Mark yanked at the root, but Emma's foot wouldn't budge. "I need a knife. I'll be back." Mark pulled his hat down on his head and ran back to the campsite while Penny stayed with Emma.

Emma rested her head on her knees. "I'm always in the middle of a mess."

"You slipped and fell. Shit happens."

Mud and water seeped through her shorts, and she shivered in the cold rain.

Mark returned with a knife and cut the root until her foot was freed. He held out his hands, and she took them and tested her weight on her foot and said, "It doesn't hurt."

They traipsed back to the tents. Mark held her elbow. When they reached the campsite, Mark said, "Change out of your wet clothes and get warm." Emma gave him a hug and thanked him.

Mark hugged her back, pulling her tightly against his body. "Sleep well," he said into her ear. His warm breath sent shivers through her body.

Penny and Emma tumbled into the tent, laughing as they stripped off their drenched layers and threw on dry clothes for bed. Emma wore Mark's boxers every night despite their large size.

"Ooh, you're soaked," said Helen as she scooted out of the way.

Once she and Penny slid into their sleeping bags, she said, "Hey, let's play two truths and a lie."

"Fun game," said Penny.

"I love games," said Helen.

"Say three things about yourself. Two truths and one lie. We guess which one is the lie," said Emma.

"Sounds easy enough," said Helen as she tapped her finger on her chin. "Let's see. I eloped, I've flown on an airplane, and I've been arrested twice."

"Ha! The lie is arrested twice," said Emma.

"Agreed," said Penny.

"The lie is I've flown on an airplane. I'm scared to death to fly."

"No way. Arrested?" said Penny.

"Yep. My husband and I protested the Vietnam War and were arrested a couple of times. We set out to save the world. We marched for civil rights; we protested the war. The sexual revolution, drugs, and rock and roll didn't jive with my parents' idea of a traditional wedding, so we eloped. I disappointed my parents when I skipped having a wedding, but we embraced the radical changes around us. I miss those times."

"Wow. You're cool! My turn," said Penny. "My three things are: I'm a virgin, I fell asleep when I took the SAT, and I can't drive."

"Ooh, tough one," said Emma. "I bet you took the SAT wide awake."

"The lie is you can't drive," said Helen.

"Yep, Helen's correct. I'm a virgin, and I fell asleep in the middle of the SAT."

"Aw, you're still a virgin," said Emma.

Penny shrugged her shoulders. "It's the reason I broke up with my boyfriend. He issued an ultimatum. Sex or end the relationship. I wasn't ready, so we broke up."

"Smart," said Helen. "Your body is your temple, and you should only invite those who worship it inside."

Emma nodded and pointed at Helen. "Penny, listen to this brilliant woman. My three things are: I've authored a book, I survived an assault, and I've run a marathon."

"Hmm," said Helen. "The lie is you've authored a book."

"I think the lie is you've run a marathon," said Penny.

"You're both wrong," said Emma. "I've lived in Chicago my whole life and never been mugged."

"Is a big city as awesome as I imagine it to be?" asked Penny.

"The restaurants and shops are great, and the professional music and sports are cool. But I must admit, I love this place. It's a ton of work to see the beauty of the Boundary Waters in person, but definitely worth it, and the wild animals are a bonus. I'm at a crossroads and now is the perfect time to change the direction of my life."

"What will you do?" asked Helen.

"I'm not sure, but I need a change."

The rain lashed the tent, and the relentless thunder and lightning crashed around them. When the women ran out of stories to tell, Penny and Helen rolled over to sleep. Emma lay awake as different ideas of ways to change her life gnawed at her. Eventually, she dozed off to the sound of the elements pummeling the earth.

Emma sipped her tea and graded papers on the quiet porch while the loons called to one another on the lake. She rocked in the soft breeze, and a car pulled up to the cabin. The car door opened, and a boot stepped onto the ground. Emma waved . . .

. . .

A crash of broken glass jerked her from the dream, and she woke in the boggy tent with Penny and Helen. The dream faded as noisy thunder and powerful winds shook the tent. Water seeped under her, and Emma shifted to avoid the wetness.

The next time Emma woke up, birds sang their songs and the sun beat down on the tent. Meanwhile, a fire raged on her butt and thighs.

"What time is it? Is it late? You're scratching. Is it chiggers?" said Penny.

"I've got a terrible itch on the back of my thighs and my ass. I can't stand it. Will you check it out?"

"Roll over."

Emma rolled onto her belly and pulled down her boxer shorts.

"Um, I don't think it's chiggers. There're trails of red on your butt and the backs of your thighs. I'll call Jim."

Emma jerked her head off the tent floor. "No! Jim can't stare at my bare butt. Get Helen," said Emma.

"Hold on."

Penny unzipped the tent. Helen was talking with Mark and Jim by the firepit.

"Hey, Helen? We need you in the tent for a minute. Emma itches, but it's not chiggers," called Penny.

"Be right there."

Helen unzipped the tent. "What's up?"

"It's Emma's backside and thighs," said Penny.

"Did you survey the ground before you squatted in the woods?"

"No, I didn't survey the ground in the storm, and I fell into a mudhole. What is it?"

"You've got poison ivy," said Helen. "There's a topical lotion and a steroid shot in the first-aid kit if it spreads."

"Oh no," Emma whined. "Poison ivy? I can't canoe with poison ivy!"

"Well, we're not canoeing today. We have bigger problems. I'll get the medicine," said Helen, and she left the tent.

"What happened?" Emma asked Penny.

Penny shrugged her shoulders.

Helen returned with the medicine, helped her apply it, and handed her new boxer shorts. "Go commando and *don't* scratch." Emma rolled her eyes, and the women exited the tent. Emma blinked in the bright sun and joined the others circled around the campfire pit.

After he documented the damage on the camera, Jim addressed the group. "As you can see, the storm created extensive damage. A loose, solo kayak washed up on our shore. Someone needs our help. We'll alter our trip today to find the owner of the kayak. We must assist others in trouble in the wilderness." Jim continued, "Tom, Helen, and I will search the lake for the owner of the lost kayak. Given the wave pattern, the kayak blew north, so we'll travel south. The rest of you will clean up the campsite and build a fire. Please check the canoes for damage and repair the tents. The wind battered the side of the men's tent and ripped a hole, and water seeped in one corner of the women's tent. Mark will direct those activities."

Emma surveyed the campsite. The wind continued its assault, and leaves and branches littered the site. Across the bay, uprooted trees dotted the shoreline. The men's tent had collapsed on one side, and a thick tree branch laid three feet from the women's tent.

Jim, Helen, and Tom ate a cold breakfast, gathered their supplies, and left to find the owner of the solo kayak. Emma and Mark hiked into the woods to gather dry wood for a fire, and Bob and Penny picked up debris around the campsite.

Emma stepped over fallen branches and mud puddles on the forest floor.

"I can't believe I have poison ivy," said Emma.

"It's a rite of passage for a camper. Now you're one of us," teased Mark.

"Great," said Emma.

Emma reached to grab a stick and tripped on a root. Mark caught her arm before she hit the ground.

"Thanks. It's slippery this morning. Can I hold on to you?"

Mark didn't answer but held his arm out to her. She grabbed it, and the jolt of heat allowed Emma to forget about the poison ivy. Her insides turned to goo as her hand slipped into the crease of his elbow.

Once back at the campsite, Penny built the fire, and they ate brunch and cleaned up. Mark and Penny repaired the tents, and everyone kept an eye out for the rest of the group's return. They finished the chores by late afternoon.

"Penny, how about a game of cribbage?" asked Bob.

Penny smiled. "Why not?" They retreated into the men's tent to play the game.

Emma found a dry log to sit on and brought it close to the fire. After he packed up the tent-repair kit, Mark joined her.

"Don't scratch."

"I can't help it, it's maddening."

"I can help you apply the lotion."

"You know where my poison ivy *is*, right?"

"Um, yeah." Mark turned every shade of red, and then he picked up a stick and peeled the bark.

Emma kicked the dust beside the fire and imagined his broad hands on the backs of her thighs and backside. Her body heated and she cleared her throat. "Are they safe out there? The churned-up lake looks dangerous, and the wind is still fierce."

"You're right. The lake is scary today, but I bet they've already found the owner of the lost kayak."

"What if they don't come back?"

"They didn't pack sleeping bags or a tent. Navigation on a lake is difficult after dark, even with head lamps, so we'll keep the fire lit. If they don't return tonight, we'll figure out a plan in the morning."

Emma hugged her knees and rocked back and forth. "I'm scared. We're in the middle of nowhere."

Mark rubbed Emma's back. "We're together and safe."

"For the moment," Emma whispered.

Chapter Twelve

"ARE THEY BACK?" asked Penny as dinnertime neared.

Mark shook his head.

"It's late," said Bob.

"Yep. If they don't return this evening, two of us will search tomorrow morning," said Mark.

Emma shook her head. "Three weeks ago, my biggest worry in life involved what color miniskirt to wear to a martini bar."

"Right?" said Penny. "But they're all experienced canoe campers. I bet they will return tonight. Anyone else hungry?"

"Always," said Emma.

"Let's cook creamy noodles and campfire toast for dinner," said Bob. "I may not be as skilled as Helen, but I've cooked a dinner or two on a campfire, and Tom isn't here to pester me."

"Excellent," said Penny.

"I'll boil the water," said Emma.

"I'll find wood to build up the fire," said Mark.

"Can you help me with the lotion before we start dinner?" Emma asked Penny.

The girls escaped into the tent.

"Can I tell you something?" asked Penny as she slathered the lotion on Emma's thighs.

"Sure."

"It stinks that someone lost their kayak, but I needed a break today. I'm sick of canoeing," admitted Penny.

"I won't tell anyone." Emma winked.

Penny capped the lotion. "Let's help Bob with dinner."

Emma retrieved water to boil while Penny readied the toast. Mark returned with a large load of wood and built up the fire. A quiet dinner followed as they listened for their friends to return. Bob and Mark washed the dishes while Penny arranged the embers in the fire to keep the leftover dinner warm.

The moon rose behind the clouds and the wind continued to blow. Tree branches swayed, and the churned-up lake splashed against the rocks. Emma slipped on a sweatshirt and found Mark by the lakeshore on a flat rock.

"It's late," she said.

Mark settled his arm around Emma's shoulders, and she leaned into him. His steady heartbeat matched hers and his smoky campfire smell comforted her. She rested her palm on his thigh and he pulled her closer.

"Emma? Where are you?" Penny yelled, running toward them. Mark and Emma flew apart from each other on the rock. Penny halted in her tracks. "Oops!" Penny giggled. "When you guys are . . . um . . . done, Bob and I want to play twenty questions, and you can join us. But it looks like you've found a better way to pass the time." Her laugh echoed over the lake as she skipped back to the firepit.

Emma groaned. "Sorry." They stood, and she peered into Mark's eyes. They shared a long look.

"It's fine. Let's play the game." They walked back to the

firepit and joined Penny and Bob. They played twenty questions for an hour while owls hooted night music.

After several rounds, Bob said, "The mosquitoes are out for their dinner. I'm hittin' the sack."

"Me too," said Penny.

"Let's monitor the fire overnight in shifts. If they are traveling in the dark, they will look for the smoke and flames from our fire," said Mark.

"I'll take the first shift. I'm itchy anyway," said Emma.

Emma applied lotion to her thighs and butt and slipped on leggings and a warm sweatshirt. She dragged her sleeping bag to the firepit and set up for the next few hours. Everyone else went to bed, and quiet ensued. She snuggled in her sleeping bag and absorbed the heat from the flames. Despite the challenges, the wilderness entranced her, and she had survived without her friends or a restaurant on every corner. She didn't miss her phone and welcomed the break from technology. Penny's spirit and Mark's kindness helped through the challenges. The safeness of Mark's arm around her shoulder was a comfort, and she closed her eyes to conjure the heaviness of his arm and his kind smile. The heat between them grew every day. The unzipping of a tent interrupted her musings.

She sat up and turned to find Mark zipping the men's tent closed. He sat beside her on the ground. Emma unzipped her bag, spread it over her legs like a blanket, and lifted the corner. Mark slipped his legs under the bag and pressed close to her. Their thighs touched and Emma gazed into his face, illuminated by moonlight.

Mark whispered, "I couldn't sleep."

"I'm glad." Emma placed her hand on top of Mark's and savored the light touch. Emma said, "Can I ask you a question?"

"Anything."

"Are you married?"

"Emma . . . Emma . . . I . . ." Mark pulled his hand from under hers and ran it across his jaw. "I'm a wid—"

A ruckus by the lakeshore interrupted them. Emma scrambled from under the sleeping bag. "Are they back?"

"Yep!"

Mark and Emma hurried to the shore to see their teammates lug the canoes onto dry land.

"You guys all right?" asked Mark.

Tom grunted and Helen said, "Hungry."

"Go up to the campsite. Dinner is warm in the firepit. Emma and I will take care of all this."

The weary travelers didn't argue. Mark and Emma tied the canoes and stored the gear while their teammates ate. No one said much due to the late hour. Once everyone had eaten and readied for bed, Mark and Emma extinguished the fire and hugged goodnight outside the tents.

The following morning, Jim recapped their adventure over breakfast. "We canoed two hours before spotting smoke from a campfire on the east side of the lake. When we approached the site, Helen called to the young man with his head in his hands. Relief shone on his face, and he broke into a wide smile. His kayak broke loose from a fallen tree in the storm. He offered us lunch and we shared the meal with him before heading back."

Tom continued with the story. "Tons of tree damage littered the lake and fierce winds pummeled the boats. We worked and worked, but two hours passed, and we didn't make much progress in the strong headwind. We didn't want to capsize, so Helen saved the day."

"I figured if we lashed our canoes to each other, we'd save each other from capsizing," said Helen.

"Ingenious," said Tom. "But we needed to tie them together. We pulled over to an island and found a downed balsa tree. We cut strips of the malleable wood, and we used them to lash the bows of the canoes together. Dusk had settled in by the time we finished. We voted and agreed to forge ahead. We didn't want to sleep in the elements on the island."

"Three miles in a headwind feels like a hundred," said Helen.

"You're exhausted, Helen. I'll portage the canoe today," said Mark in his quiet, deep voice.

Emma smiled at the kindness he showed toward his canoe partner, and a memory of Craig stopped her in her tracks.

Emma taught first grade all day and stayed late for parent-teacher conferences. Upon her arrival home, after nine, she received a call from the hospital that her dad had been injured in a minor car accident. She hopped back into her car and drove to the hospital to find her mother yelling at the nurse and her dad pale as a ghost after the doctor reset his arm. The paperwork nightmare and running interference between the staff and her mother sapped the rest of her energy. Craig was on his phone when she arrived home after one in the morning. He found her in the bathroom brushing her teeth. "Hey, hope your dad is all right. We're having friends over for dinner tomorrow night."

Emma grimaced. "I don't want to host a dinner party tomorrow night. Besides, we don't have any food and the house is cluttered. Tomorrow's a school day and I don't have time to plan for it. Call them back and cancel."

"Nope. Dinner is at eight. Figure it out."

She crawled into bed and cried silent tears into the pillow.

After breakfast cleanup, Emma listened to the daily instructions. "To make up for time lost, we'll paddle twelve miles and hike three portages today," said Jim. "Once we reach our campsite for the night, we'll stay for two days. It's a gorgeous setting, and the perfect place to regroup for the final portion of our trip."

The team broke camp and reloaded the canoes. Jim, adamant to leave no human trace, scoured the campsite for debris. The weather cooperated with a mild temperature and no wind. The easy paddle to the first portage buoyed the teams' spirits. But, once they unloaded the gear and started to hike, their enthusiasm waned. Rain and debris from the storm filled the low-lying path and created a mudhole on the trail.

"This sucks," groaned Penny.

Emma squelched and squished along, lifting her hiking boot out of a muddy hole and splashing her calves with mud. Her heavy boots slowed down the pace of the portage, and Penny's incessant whining didn't help. The fresh mud smell soured her stomach, and wet tree branches slapped her face. After the two-hour slog through the woods, thick mud covered Emma's legs up to her knees. Emma, Mark, and Tom retrieved the second load of gear, and by the time they reached the end of the trail, Emma's thighs burned.

She joined the team and knocked the caked mud from her boots.

"The sun will dry the mud," said Helen. "Whatever you do, don't dip your boots in water."

"But they're *heavy*," Penny whined in a singsong voice.

"They'll be heavier if you get them wet," retorted Helen.

A small lake welcomed the group and featured a large island encircled by birds.

"What are those birds?" asked Emma.

"Those are turkey vultures," said Bob. "They're feastin' on somethin'."

As the team approached the tiny island, Penny said, "Oh no, a baby moose!"

Emma wrinkled her nose when the wind blew. "Let's go."

The next two portages proved easy, and the dirty crew paddled their boats onto a small beach at the campsite in the late afternoon.

"Tough day, but great job. This campsite is one of my favorites. We'll camp here for two days to regroup for the final leg of our trip," announced Jim.

Birch trees ringed the campsite and flat rocks jutted into the lake on the north side of the area. The teams lined their muddy boots on one of the rocks and pitched the tents on a large flat space. A carpet of white wildflowers trailed into the woods, and the large size of the campsite allowed for the group to spread out. Jim captured the muddy boots on film, as well as the pairs of campers who pitched the tents. Bob and Tom promised fish tomorrow and cooked another freeze-dried meal for dinner. After everyone completed dinner chores, Bob and Tom told scary ghost stories around the firepit. Emma tuned them out and waited for everyone to go to bed. Once the group retired for the night, Emma and Mark stayed by the campfire, and the flames licked the sky.

"You pushed hard today. You're a strong woman," Mark stated as he picked up her hand and rubbed her knuckles.

"Strong? I'm not strong."

"You're on this massive trip, and you've had chiggers *and* poison ivy. You've slept on the ground for the first time in your life, and you volunteered to go back for gear on the hardest portage yet. You're strong."

"My mother would disagree."

"What did your mother say when you told her about the trip?"

"I never told her. She thinks I'm lounging in a lodge for two weeks with the biggest sacrifice being no pool."

Emma giggled as Mark threw his head back and laughed.

The moon illuminated their faces and bathed the campsite in soft light.

Emma dug deep for confidence. "My lousy luck with men is legendary, and I need to ask you a question."

Mark furrowed his brow.

"Are you married?"

Mark breathed, pulled his arms away from her, and rested his elbows on his knees. "I'm a widower."

Emma inhaled a breath. She rested her hand on his bicep. "I'm sorry."

"Yeah."

They sat in silence as the fire fizzled and the moon went behind a cloud.

Chapter Thirteen

THE BREAKFAST DISHES were piled on the forest floor between Emma and Bob. Emma scrubbed the same spot on a bowl over and over again, lost in thought. A widower. On the one hand, he wasn't married. But, on the other hand, Mark's marriage didn't end by choice. Did he still love her?

"Emma? C'mon. Hand me the dish. Tom and I wanna get on the lake and fish."

"Sorry." Emma passed him the bowl and finished the plates. They hauled everything back to the campsite and went their separate ways. Jim reviewed the maps and napped, and Helen and Penny departed for a hike. Emma stored her book in her pack and strolled through the cool woods to search for wildflowers. Water splashed from a secluded cove around a bend. Emma hurried to the rock ledge to get a glimpse of the animal and stopped dead in her tracks.

Mark bathed in the cove, alone. His shoulders dripped lake water, and he wet his hair with his eyes closed. He tipped his head back into the water and drops beaded on his chest. She turned away and hurried down the path away from the rock ledge. A braver woman would strip naked and jump into the lake with him. But, she was not that girl. The path led her back to the firepit, and she retreated into the tent for a nap.

Bob and Tom returned with a load of smallmouth bass and northern pike for dinner. Jim took a picture of them with their catch. Helen cleaned the fish and washed the blood off the rocks.

Emma attempted campfire pot bread under Helen's direction. She mixed water, flour, and yeast in a small pot. She let it rise, then cooked it over the embers of the fire. The homey smell of fresh fish and warm pot bread attracted everyone to the campfire and a relaxed dinner ensued.

Penny led the group in songs around the campfire after dinner. The group sang as the sun fell behind the trees. Darkness followed, and Emma pressed her shoulder and leg against Mark's. One by one, the team retired for the night, but Emma stayed by the fire. Mark picked up her hand and rubbed his thumb across her knuckles. Butterflies took flight in her belly, and she gazed into his eyes. Mark brushed his plump, wet lips against her thin lips and they held still in the kiss. When he pulled back, she sighed and opened her eyes. She cupped his chin and thumbed the thick stubble. She pulled him toward her and brought his lips to hers again. Her core liquified and her sex pulsed when he flicked his tongue against her lips. Mark slipped a hand behind her neck and tugged the band out of her ponytail. Her hair tumbled into his hand and he threaded his fingers through her waves. Their tongues danced to their own beat and when they came up for a breath, Mark breathed in raspy shallow breaths and pressed his forehead to hers.

"I love to kiss you, but I don't . . ." A rustle sounded. Mark held still and lifted his head.

"What's the matter?" Emma whispered.

"Shh."

Emma followed the noise and pointed as the color drained from her face. Mark covered her mouth with his hand to stifle her scream. A black bear stood, three feet tall on four legs, snorting and sniffing around the tree fifteen feet from the firepit. He paced around the tree and angled his head toward the food bag. The bear stood on two legs and growled and scratched at the tree. He paced back and forth and roared. The bear turned and galloped away from the campsite, and then stopped and turned back. When the animal charged toward them, Emma shrieked and Mark grabbed a pot and a pan and banged them together. The noise echoed through the forest and bounced off the lake. The bear roared, standing up on two legs. Then, he thumped back to the ground and, on all fours, snorted and ambled into the woods.

Emma's knees knocked together and her body shook. Mark dropped the pot and the pan and wrapped his arms around her. "Breathe."

She bowed her head between her knees and tried to catch her breath. "Shit, shit, shit."

"He smelled the food bag or the fish we ate for dinner. It's why you hang the food high. Boundary Water bears love human food."

Jim popped his head out of the tent. "Bear?"

"Yep. He's gone."

"Are you okay, Emma?" asked Jim.

Emma scowled at Jim, and he retreated into the tent. Mark rubbed her back until her breath slowed.

Mark held her tight, and she leaned against his shoulder. "You're safe."

Emma shook her head and willed her heart to slow.

Mark grinned. "I'll stay with you until the adrenaline wears off. Breathe."

. . .

The following morning, Emma kept one eye over her shoulder, expecting the bear to return while the team ate breakfast. Mark recounted the tale of the bear. Jim praised them for correct behavior and told the group, "If another bear visits, bang pots and pans together and they will scamper away from the loud noise." He snapped a picture of the group at breakfast. "Rest, relax, and gear up for the end of the trip."

Emma and Penny hiked after breakfast in the shade of the cool forest.

"So, what's goin' on with Mark?"

Emma kicked a rock and debated how much to share with Penny. "Um, he saved me from the bear. We talk. He told me he's a widower."

"Wow. Heavy news."

"I know. He's too young to be a widower. He's sweet and helpful, but a widower carries baggage."

"So does a divorcée."

"Touché. Come on, let's head back."

The girls went left on the trail to return to the campsite. They talked and walked for another hour, but the campsite didn't appear.

"Hey, where's the campsite?" asked Emma.

Penny and Emma stopped and surveyed the area. They turned in circles to locate the sun through a break in the dense canopy.

"Are we lost?" asked Penny.

"No, we can't be lost," said Emma.

"My parents will kill me if I die in the woods," said Penny.

"We won't die in the woods."

"Are you sure? What if we starve or get eaten by a bear?"

Emma shuddered. "Let's not talk about bears."

. . .

Mark skipped rocks by the lake and contemplated Emma. She was a tiny person with a personality the size of the Grand Canyon. Her tasty lips and tongue stirred his dormant sex drive. He was attracted to her, but was he ready for a relationship? He skipped a rock, and it sank in the water. He bent down and found another rock. Emma lived six hundred miles away from him and had friends and a career in Chicago. He skipped the rock and it bumped once and sank. A larger, flatter rock captured his attention. The smoothness of the rock between his fingers reminded him of Emma's silky skin. He rubbed it over and over, like he wanted to stroke Emma. He skipped it into the water, and it bumped four times over the calm lake. Satisfied, he headed back toward the campsite to find Emma and ask her to go for a hike. Tom whittled a stick and Helen worked on her crossword by the firepit.

"Where are Emma and Penny?" asked Mark.

"They went for a hike after breakfast," said Tom.

Mark frowned. "We ate breakfast over three hours ago. I'll look for them. I doubt they meant to be gone this long."

"I'll help," said Helen.

Helen put a couple of granola bars in her pocket and Mark grabbed water and a compass. They headed into the woods.

Mark cupped his hands over his mouth and bellowed, "*Em*-ma! *Pen*-ny!"

"The trees are dense here. It would be easy to get lost," said Helen.

"You're right. Let's leave some markers along the trail to find our way back." Mark pulled a bandana from his pocket and tied it to a tree.

"Penny, Emma!" Helen called.

"I'm thirsty," said Penny.

"Me too. We're so stupid. We didn't even bring water! Should we walk or wait here until someone finds us?" asked Emma.

"I don't know." Penny leaned back against a tree and snapped her fingers. "Wait. I remember my dad told me moss grows on the north side of trees. So, if we figure out which way the campsite is, we'll find our way back by the moss on the trees."

"That sounds pretty far-fetched, and besides, which way is the campsite?" asked Emma.

Penny hugged her knees. "We're *lost*."

Emma slapped a spider crawling up her leg. "I know," she whispered.

They stayed in place and stared at each other with widened eyes.

Another half-hour passed, and Emma bit her bottom lip and paced the forest floor holding her stomach.

"Oh no! Are you going to throw up?" Penny ran up to her and eased her onto a log. She rubbed her back.

"No, just nauseous." She took deep breaths and counted back from one hundred to distract herself from her soured belly.

"Maybe someone will look for us," said Penny.

"We should stay here. I think our chances of being found are better if we don't move."

"Okay." Penny slid off the log onto the ground and stacked stones.

A rustle sounded, and Emma jumped. A squirrel scampered up a tree, and her shoulders sagged.

A little while later, Penny said, "Hey, listen."

"I don't hear anything."

"Shh."

Penny jumped up from the ground. "I hear Mark's voice!" Penny cupped her hands around her mouth and shouted, "Mark!"

"Emma?" Helen's voice floated over the canopy.

"Helen?" shouted Emma.

"Stay where you are and yell!" said Helen.

Helen and Mark jogged through the dense forest toward them a few minutes later. Emma stood and relief washed over her as they approached. Mark opened his arms and engulfed Emma in a hug. "You're safe." Mark pulled Emma tightly into his arms and kissed the top of her head.

Helen and Penny exchanged a look and smiled at Mark and Emma.

"What happened?" asked Helen.

"We got lost," said Penny.

"We didn't plan on a long hike, but we got turned around in the dense trees," said Emma.

Helen handed the water to Penny, and she passed it to Emma.

"Let's head back to the campsite," said Helen.

Mark headed down to the lake, passing Helen resting in a hammock she'd made from a tent fly and cattails. Jim snuck a few snapshots of the hammock and Bob and Tom's cribbage game.

Mark doodled with a stick in the sand on the beach. A loon family hunted for dinner and birds sang overhead. The cool breeze blew his T-shirt, and the sun warmed his face. He smiled when Helen sat beside him.

"Cool hammock," said Mark.

"A trick I learned years ago. Penny wanted a turn."

Mark nodded.

"Recovered from the bear experience yet?" asked Helen.

Mark nodded. "I've encountered bears before. But our bear was huge! I hid my fear from Emma."

"So, are you two a couple?"

Mark angled his face to the sky and searched for answers in the wispy clouds. "I like her a lot, but I haven't dated anyone since Meg died." Mark faced Helen. "Did you feel guilty dating after your husband died?"

"Life is long and you're a young man. There's no shame in falling in love again. Emma is a gem, and you belong together. The energy and the intensity you share is palpable." Helen patted his knee and walked away.

It wasn't until after she'd left that he realized Helen never answered his question.

Chapter Fourteen

THE TWO DAYS OFF rejuvenated the group, and Emma helped break camp the next morning. She'd survived two thirds of the trip, but Jim had planned a long, hard day with two portages and warned them about steep terrain on the first portage.

Bob and Tom collapsed the men's tent and rolled it into its pack.

"I'll carry it to the shore," said Tom.

"I've got it," said Bob.

"No, give it to me, I'm headed down there anyway."

The men yanked on the tent until Tom let go and said, "Fine, you take it."

Bob pulled hard on the tent and the momentum tossed him backward into Emma. Bob and Emma collapsed in a heap on the ground. White-hot pain shot through her eye, and she yelled, "Aargh!" She covered her left eye with her hand and winced.

Bob scrambled off Emma and the group ran over to them.

"Are you hurt?" Mark extended his hand to Emma and

helped her sit up. She kept her palm over her eye, and a bump emerged on her forehead. Penny ran to retrieve the first-aid kit.

"Sorry," said Bob. "It was Tom's fault. He let go of the tent and I fell."

"*My* fault? Are you crazy, old man?" asked Tom.

"Enough!" demanded Jim. "Gentlemen, we're done. Your quarrels stop *now*. Understood?"

The men grumbled as Penny returned with the first-aid kit. She opened the kit, pulled out a cold pack, and squeezed it to activate the contents. Emma placed the pack on her eye and forehead and blew out a long breath.

Bob and Tom glared at each other while Jim evaluated Emma for signs of concussion. Her eye swelled and the bump turned purple.

The team dispersed to load the canoes, but Mark stayed with Emma.

"I can't believe those idiots! Can you paddle today?"

"I'm fine. Thanks. I think a tent pole hit my face when Bob fell into me."

"Keep the ice on it as long as you can while we break camp," said Mark.

Jim delayed their departure by an hour for Emma to recover. Once on the lake, Penny and Emma hung behind the group and canoed near shore to capture the shade. A fish jumped out of the water in front of them, and Penny screamed and waved her paddle in the air. They rocked back and forth until the canoe leaned so far to the left, the packs hit the water and the canoe capsized.

Emma kicked her sodden boots in the murky water and sputtered as she and Penny righted the canoe and pushed it to the shore. She heaved her waterlogged body out of the lake and stood on the bank. The life jacket landed on the rock with a thud, and she squeezed water out of her hair. Ugh, wet socks and undies sucked in a canoe.

"Sorry. The fish startled me." Penny twisted the water out of her shirt and shook her hair.

The other teams paddled back to the sodden girls. Emma pulled her wet T-shirt off and stood on the rocks in a sports bra. She wrung out the T-shirt and slipped it back on over her head, wincing as it brushed the bump on her forehead.

Jim said, "Girls, what happened? Are you all right?"

"We're fine. A fish jumped and startled Penny, and we lost our balance," said Emma.

Bob and Tom helped to load the wet, heavy packs back into the canoe and Emma held the boat for Penny and climbed in behind her. Her wet clothes clung to her body and she shivered in the breeze. A steady throb pulsed behind her eye. She wasn't looking forward to the tough portage up ahead.

Their paddle rhythm returned, and Penny muttered, "Sorry."

The beauty of the lakes settled Emma, and she paddled while her clothes dried in the hot sun. Her thoughts drifted to her home life. She needed a change, but what? A larger, more affordable apartment complex would save her money, but the lengthy commute gave her pause. Besides, what better place to live than across the street from Lake Michigan with its beaches and parks? She despised the crowded train but relished the convenience of it. A gentle breeze blew as they rounded a corner in the lake, and she debated a move away from Chicago. Northern Minnesota would be cheaper than the city, and the slower pace of life appealed to her. But she would miss her girl-friends and her school. That said, she wouldn't run into Craig's new family. Did she have the courage to move away from Chicago and her secure job?

Penny pointed. "Hey, everyone stopped."

Emma slowed the canoe. "The lake is blocked."

A large beaver dam blocked the river they needed to travel to the first portage. Jim opened his pack and pulled out the camera to take a picture.

"How do we get past it?" asked Emma.

"We get out of our canoes and pull them over the dam. The gear stays in the hull," said Helen.

Jim got out of his canoe and stood in two feet of water. He grabbed the bow and pulled the canoe over the dam. The rest of the team followed him. Emma and Penny worked together to pull their canoe across the dam with the heavy gear in the hull. Their near-dry clothes got soaked for the second time. As soon as everyone crossed the dam and settled into their respective canoes, they continued down the river. The river flowed quickly, and the canoe pulled from side to side. Emma's biceps burned as she steered the boat through the rapids. Ducks, herons, and other birds inhabited the area, and the noise from their flocks hindered conversation until they reached the portage.

Emma carried the canoe for the portage and, at one point, tipped the bow onto the ground to rest.

"You all right?" asked Penny.

Emma held the weight of the canoe on her shoulders and shook her arms. "My head throbs and these hills are tough."

"Let me portage the canoe," said Penny as she dumped the pack onto the ground.

The girls brought the canoe to the ground and rested. Emma wiped the sweat off her face with the hem of her T-shirt, and Penny gathered her hair and whipped it into a messy braid.

Penny pointed. "There's a boulder up ahead, let's each grab

an end of the canoe and walk it over the boulder. I don't want to slip on the rock with the canoe on my head."

"Good idea. Let's go."

The girls carried the canoe over the boulder, returned for the pack, and finished the horrendous portage.

Mark, Bob, and Jim volunteered for the second trip to carry the rest of the gear. Once everyone completed the portage, the team broke for lunch on the large, flat rocks at the exit.

"Jim, pass me an antacid," said Helen.

"Sure," said Jim. He dug into the first-aid kit. "Here you go. Indigestion?"

"Heartburn."

Penny told stories from college while they ate lunch, and Bob's laughter echoed through the forest. Emma sat against a tree and rested. Her head pounded and her eye hurt, she smelled, and her dirty shorts had a tear in the hem, but Mark caught her eye and gave her a lusty look. She batted her eyelashes and wet her lips. The fierce desire to be with him skin to skin consumed her. "Emma?" asked Jim. "You're red in the face. Do you need water? Be careful you don't dehydrate."

"I'm fine, sorry. I love to daydream."

Mark grinned his half smile at Emma and winked. They locked eyes and it took every ounce of willpower not to leap into his arms and kiss him.

"Let's move. It's dark to the west," said Helen.

"You're right," said Jim. "Let's go."

Chapter Fifteen

CLOUDS ROLLED IN, and the afternoon gave way to a steady rain. The absence of thunder and lightning allowed the team to continue, but the portage proved muddy and everyone became drenched and dirty. Jim announced names of lakes and portages, but Emma didn't listen. She focused on the paddle.

"Hey everyone, how does a macaroni-and-cheese dinner sound?" asked Bob.

"Divine," said Penny.

The slippery ground forced the team to work together to raise both tents. They were securing the women's tent when a smack startled Emma and she dropped her tent pole. "Sorry. Did I hear a gunshot?" Emma asked with wide eyes.

"I bet we interrupted a beaver," said Jim. He surveyed the perimeter of the site. "Over there." He pointed. "Check out the baby pine tree by the shore. It's half-eaten."

"Lots of beavers today." Helen rubbed her arm.

"Does your arm hurt, Helen?" asked Emma.

"Yep. I pulled it on the portage. I'll be fine. Thanks."

The rain reduced to a drizzle an hour later and everyone

changed out of their wet clothes. Against all odds, Emma found a clean T-shirt in her pack. Penny tossed dirty clothes around the tent and hunted for dry socks.

"We need dry wood to build a fire for dinner. Who wants to fetch some?" asked Mark.

"I'll go," said Tom.

"Emma, will you help me tie down the canoes?" asked Mark.

She nodded and followed Mark to the shore.

Mark held the canoe while Emma tied the knots and secured the boat to a tree. Movement in the swampy area to the left of the shore caught her eye. "Hey, look." She pointed. Emma inhaled as two graceful birds picked through the cove. "What are they?"

"Herons. Those two are mates."

She crossed her arms and sighed. "This place is awesome. I'll miss it."

"I camp as often as I can. I love it here." Mark moved beside Emma, and she leaned into him, nestling her head into the perfect curve of his shoulder. His body warmed her, and her heart skipped a beat when he smiled.

"I might move out of the city," said Emma.

"Do you live downtown?"

"Yeah. I live in a studio apartment on the lakeshore. The lake and parks are great, but the noise is relentless."

"You like the quiet in the Boundary Waters."

"I do." She laughed. "Maybe I should live up here in the middle of nowhere."

The herons picked through the marsh as Mark pulled Emma tighter.

Emma held Mark's hand as they walked up the path to the firepit. The clouds parted and the sky brightened.

"Look, a rainbow!" shouted Penny. "Make a wish!"

"Clear skies," said Bob.

"Dry socks," said Penny.

"Answers," said Emma.

Mark returned from a bathroom break in the woods and joined the rest of the group as they huddled around the campfire.

"Well done, Bob. The mac and cheese hit the spot. Thanks," said Emma.

"Helen, you didn't eat much," said Jim.

Helen pressed a hand against her chest. "My heartburn flared after dinner yesterday. I'm ready for bed. Goodnight everyone."

Penny taught the group the "never have I ever" game, and they talked and laughed around the fire for the next hour. Mark kneaded Emma's shoulders throughout the game. His heart beat fast and the heat from Emma's body tightened his muscles. One by one, the group retired and left Emma and Mark alone.

"Chilly?" asked Mark.

"Uh huh."

Mark moved from the log to the ground behind Emma. "Come closer."

Emma scooted back and leaned her head against Mark's shoulder while he crossed his arms around her. His forearms grazed her breasts, and she pressed her body into his hardness as they held each other.

"Does your eye hurt?"

"My head hurts, but my eye is okay."

Mark's hands roamed from Emma's torso to the curve of her

breast as he nuzzled her neck. Emma turned her head and accepted his kiss. Their union sparked passion and she turned to straddle him. She linked her arms around his neck and settled into his lap to kiss him. They kissed and kissed until their lips moved as one. Like a drug, Mark was hooked and didn't want to stop. After a breath, their lips met again and this time the kisses went from feather light to heady passion. Mark kissed her neck and worked his way to an earlobe, and he pulled it between his lips. Emma purred and slid her hands under his T-shirt, running her smooth hands along the hard planes of his chest to finger his chest hair. He followed her lead and reached under her shirt and brushed his thumb across the front of her bra and over her stiff nipple. When Emma ground against Mark's hardness, he held her still. "We're not alone."

"I know," whispered Emma.

They stood up and regarded each other. Mark brought Emma into his embrace and caressed her cheek. After another long, deep kiss, they parted.

After days on the lakes, the ripe smell in the tent woke Emma at sunrise. She climbed out of the tent and stretched her arms up to the sky to loosen the muscles in her back, tight from sleeping on the ground. The tents stayed quiet, so she walked to the lake and sat on the rocky shore. She hugged her knees and rubbed her arms as loon families swam in the lake and dove for their breakfast. She picked up a stick and doodled in the pebbles. Her chest fluttered when she remembered how Mark had grazed his thumb over her nipples pressed tight against her bra. The hard planes of his chest and tight stomach filled her with desire and her body warmed. The sun rose higher and voices from the campsite carried over the water. She erased her scribbles and joined the group at the firepit.

· · ·

Emma and Penny trekked to the woods to pee and stumbled upon Helen, bent over and vomiting.

"Helen?" shouted Penny.

"I'm fine. Don't worry about me."

"I'll tell Jim. We can hang here today if you're ill," said Emma. She ran back to the firepit. "Jim!" she called.

Jim secured his pack on the ground and regarded Emma. "Helen's sick. I think we should stay here today."

"What's wrong?"

"She vomited in the woods."

Helen and Penny approached the campsite. "I'm fine," said Helen.

Jim stood and asked Helen, "Are you sure?"

"I'm sure. Lots of miles to cover today."

"You'll let me know if we need to stop?"

"Of course."

Emma kept an eye on Helen while they broke camp. Her pale face didn't stop her efforts. She collapsed the tent and loaded gear into the canoes with the rest of them. The still lake allowed for fast boats, but oppressive heat blanketed the area by late morning. Emma monitored Helen as they paddled.

The next portage began with a steep climb and the team groaned. They unloaded the gear, and pairs hiked the trail. Penny portaged their canoe and Emma followed with the pack. Helen brought up the rear as usual. Emma was maneuvering around a large rock when a crash sounded behind her. Emma whipped around. Helen lay face down on the ground, pinned under her canoe.

Chapter Sixteen

"HELEN!" Emma screamed. She dropped her pack on the trail and ran back to her. She heaved the canoe off Helen and turned her body over.

"Penny, Penny!" Emma yelled as she checked for a pulse. "Penny, come back!"

"What happened?" shouted Penny from the trail.

Helen's pulse beat under Emma's fingers. "Helen fainted. Go get everyone, and bring the first-aid kit!"

Emma shook her. "Helen, wake up."

Helen blinked her eyes open and winced when she touched the back of her head. "What happened?"

"I think your heart is giving you trouble, and you fainted. The canoe bumped your head and knocked you out."

"There's nothing wrong with my heart." Helen moved to sit up.

Emma stopped her. "You complained of indigestion and a sore left arm yesterday. You vomited this morning. You need a doctor."

Heavy footfalls approached the scene. Jim sank down beside Emma and tossed the first-aid kit onto the ground.

"What happened?"

"Helen was carrying the canoe up the hill and I think she fainted and hit her head. Her pulse is thready and she's pale. I think she's having heart problems. How close are we to civilization?"

"We're a day and a half from the lodge. We need an emergency seaplane."

Helen sat up. "No way. I'm fine. I'm not going on any plane."

Jim fished an aspirin out of the first-aid kit and handed it to Helen. "Take the aspirin. Emma's right. You need to get to a hospital."

Helen scowled but swallowed the aspirin and flopped back onto the ground.

Jim addressed the group. "I'll paddle the solo canoe to high ground and use the satellite phone to call for a seaplane. You need to get Helen to the portage exit, monitor her, and wait for the plane. Tom, come with me and help me pack."

Jim and Tom jogged down the half-mile trail toward the portage exit with the solo canoe, Jim's pack, and the food. They loaded the canoe with his pack, filtered water, and one meal's worth of food. "Tom, the priority is to keep Helen alive. Wait for the seaplane. Don't leave the portage until I return." Jim crossed his fingers. "With luck, I'll beat the plane."

"Be safe. Good luck," said Tom as Jim paddled away.

Tom jogged back to the team. Emma hovered over Helen, Penny paced, and Mark wrung his hands.

"Jim is off to find high ground so the satellite phone will work," said Tom. "We need to solve several problems. First, we need to move the canoes and gear to the portage exit. Then, we need to clear an area for tents at the exit and move Helen off the trail and into a tent. Emma, stay with Helen. Everyone else, let's haul the canoes and gear to the portage exit."

Tom grabbed Helen's canoe and Penny ran ahead to finish the portage with hers. Bob started up the trail to retrieve the gear they'd dropped. Emma kept a hand on Helen's wrist to monitor her heartbeat and frowned at Mark, frozen in place. "Mark? Go. Finish the portage and then come back."

"Right."

An hour passed before the team returned to Helen and Emma.

"How is she?" asked Mark as he crouched beside Emma on the trail.

"Ornery. You're as pale as a ghost."

"This is scary."

"You're right. Can you take off your shirt and set it under Helen's head? These small rocks are sharp."

"Yeah, sure." Mark removed his T-shirt, folded it, and placed it under Helen's head. "Helen, hang in there. Help is on the way."

"I'm *fine*," insisted Helen.

"You aren't fine," answered Mark. "But relax and breathe. Help is on the way."

Helen closed her eyes and rested.

Mark addressed the group. "We moved the canoes and gear. We need to transport Helen to the exit. Any ideas?"

Helen sat up. "I can walk."

"No. It's a half-mile portage with steep hills," said Mark.

Helen flopped back onto the ground.

"How's about a chair-carry?" suggested Bob.

"The trail is tight in spots," said Penny.

"Penny's right. I'll carry her on my back," said Mark.

"It's far for a back-carry," said Tom.

"How 'bout we build a stretcher with a tent fly or sleeping bag and tree branches?" asked Penny. "Like the hammock."

Mark nodded and snapped his fingers. "Brilliant. Bob and Tom, can you build the stretcher? Emma, stay here with Helen. Penny, come with me to scope out a campsite and pitch a tent at the exit."

Everyone ran in different directions while Emma stayed by Helen's side.

Penny sank down on the ground near the lake and coughed. "Give me a minute." She dipped her hands into the lake, cupped water in them, and splashed it on her face. "Do you think she had a heart attack?"

"I have no idea." Mark glanced around the portage exit.

"I thought the Boundary Waters was a no-fly zone?"

"It's a no-fly zone for commercial aircraft. Emergency seaplanes are allowed."

"What should we do first?" asked Penny.

"Clear a space for the tents so when Helen arrives, we can slide her right in."

Penny nodded and they got to work.

Back at the emergency scene, Emma slapped a deerfly on her neck and monitored Helen's pulse and labored breaths. She cleared a spot to sit on the trail.

Tom and Bob returned to the scene with saplings, cattails, and a sleeping bag. They worked together to build the stretcher.

"Shoot, one of us needs to get the multi-tool from the pack to cut holes in the sleeping bag," said Tom.

"No worries, I've got my pocketknife. It'll work." Bob dug into his pocket for the knife.

Tom snapped open the pocketknife and cut two small holes in the bag's bottom. Then they threaded the long limbs through the holes. Bob lashed another sapling across the top for head support.

"Emma, lay on the stretcher to test it out," said Tom.

She lay on the stretcher, and the men lifted her into the air. "My head dips. Can you add a support beam?"

Tom nodded and Bob left to fetch saplings to shore up the head and strengthen the middle section of the stretcher.

Mark and Penny returned with water.

"How goes it at the exit?" asked Emma.

"One tent is pitched. We'll help get Helen to the exit and then pitch the other tent and dig a hole for a fire." Mark handed Emma the water.

"Thanks," Emma said as she accepted the water and helped Helen drink. Helen lay back down, and Emma stood and pulled Mark off to the side of the trail. She held his elbow. "This is my fault."

"What?"

"Helen vomited in the woods this morning. She complained of a sore left arm and heartburn. Her symptoms all point to a heart attack. I should have insisted we stay at the site this morning." Emma stifled a sob and rested her forehead on Mark's chest.

"This is not your fault, and don't think for one minute you had any control over what happened. Her symptoms also mimicked stomach upset and a pulled muscle." Mark held Emma's shoulders and pushed her back to look into her eyes. "We'll get through this together." Mark wiped away her tears and kissed her forehead.

. . .

Once Bob returned with the wood, the men stabilized the head and supported the middle of the stretcher. Tom nodded. "It's ready."

Helen lay on the stretcher and folded her arms across her chest. "I can walk, you know." No one responded. The men lifted Helen and trekked to the portage exit. Emma picked up Mark's T-shirt and followed the group.

Emma held the tent door open while Tom and Bob slid Helen inside. She climbed in behind her and handed her a bottle of water while the rest of the team cleared another area for the second tent and dug a firepit hole on the beach.

Bob left to search for dry wood while the rest of the group gaped at one another around the firepit.

After Penny built the fire, Tom said, "Let's cook dinner. We didn't eat lunch, and it's close to dinnertime."

"I'll help," said Penny.

Tom filtered the water and Penny prepared a simple freeze-dried meal for the group. Mark unzipped the tent to check on Helen and Emma. "How is she?"

"Her pulse is thready and her breaths are shallow."

"How are you?"

Emma wiped her tears and shook her head.

Mark squeezed Emma's shoulder. "Helen is in a tent and Penny cooked dinner. I'm sure we'll hear a plane soon."

Penny poked her head into the tent. "Food is ready. Emma, want a break? I can sit with Helen while you eat."

"No, but I need to use the woods. Give me five minutes." Emma left the tent.

"Mark?" Helen whispered, pulling Mark's T-shirt.

Mark leaned down close to Helen. "Yeah?"

"I'm scared to fly."

"It's a short flight back to the lodge and then they'll take you in an ambulance from there."

"But . . . can't I lay in a canoe and paddle back?"

Mark shook his head. "Sorry. We're a day and a half from the lodge, and there are portages."

Helen closed her eyes and a tear leaked out onto her cheek.

"When will the plane arrive?" asked Penny in between bites of food.

"Accordin' to the map, Jim needed to travel to the next lake and then climb a steep portage. He'll call from there. I think we'll hear a plane soon."

"I agree," said Mark. "I'll pack Helen's dry pack. We'll need to reorganize the gear in the boats."

"Yep. Tom and I'll figure it out," said Bob.

They cleaned up dinner and dipped into the lake to cool off from the hot day.

Emma remained with Helen in the tent and the rest of the team divided up the shifts to monitor the fire. Tom took the first fire shift as the sun set.

Mark entered the tent with Emma and Helen. "Bob and I gathered enough wood to get us through the night. What do you need?"

Emma sniffed her shirt and recoiled. "Can you fetch my dry pack?" she asked.

"Sure."

Mark retrieved her dry pack and left her alone in the tent to change and help Helen.

Darkness had settled over the campsite when a whirring sound rumbled in the distance. Mark jumped up and ran down to the beach. A light blinked in the sky and the plane descended onto the water. The propeller slowed, and Mark ran back to the firepit. "Plane's here. Let's get Helen to the beach."

Bob and Tom carried Helen to the beach on the stretcher. Mark carried her dry pack and the group gathered at the edge of the lake. The plane hovered near shore as the two paramedics hopped from the float into the water. Bob and Tom passed Helen to the medics over the water.

"I don't want to fly," whimpered Helen.

"I know. It'll be quick. See you soon." Mark squeezed her hand and gave the paramedic her dry pack. The team sat on the beach as the seaplane taxied over the water and flew into the black sky. The others dispersed, and Mark put his arm around Emma. She relaxed into his shoulder as the plane faded into the night.

Mark sighed and scrubbed his hand through his hair. Emma touched his arm, and the warmth of her hand and the softness of her hair along his chin encouraged him to pull back and look into her pleading eyes.

"Talk to me," said Emma.

He pulled his arm from around Emma and folded his hands in his lap. He blew out a breath and stared into the black night. "After two years of marriage, my wife, Meg, and I wanted a baby, but Meg's doctor found a lump in her breast during a routine exam." Emma rubbed his back. "Meg endured a mammogram, biopsy, and a million other tests. The cancer spread to the lymph nodes, and she suffered through a mastectomy. She came home with drains and bandages, and I helped her recuperate after surgery. The surgical recovery sucked, but the treatment made the surgery look easy." Tears pooled in his eyes but didn't fall.

"Rounds of chemo and then radiation took months. She lost all her hair and a ton of weight. The pain consumed her. But the worst news came after the PET scan. The cancer had spread to other organs and to her bones. The doctors told us to plan for palliative care. We exhausted all our treatment options. I took leave from work and brought hospice into our home. She went from a vibrant, assertive woman to a frail skeleton of her old self. She died on a bright, sunny April afternoon while I held her hand."

"Your soulmate passed and left you behind," said Emma.

Mark picked up Emma's hands, locked eyes with her, and said, "But what I don't understand is, how can Meg be my soulmate if I have this powerful desire for you?"

Chapter Seventeen

Emma opened her mouth to answer, but a blinking headlight on the lake interrupted her. She pointed. "Look! It's Jim!"

"Whew! Glad he's back safe and sound."

The team helped Jim unload his canoe and fixed him dinner. "Sleep in tomorrow. It's been a long day. Good work, everyone," said Jim.

Emma and Penny retired to their tent. "I hope Helen is all right," said Penny.

"I think she was more afraid of the plane ride than a possible heart attack," said Emma.

Penny giggled. "Truth."

Mark trailed the team on the sun-scorched lake the following afternoon. Paddling the canoe by himself slowed his pace. Jim announced another hour-long paddle before the campsite, and the group groaned. Emma wept. "I don't think I can do it," she whispered.

Mark pulled his canoe beside Emma and squeezed her shoulders. "You've canoed this far. You can do it. Let's drink some water and eat a snack before we head west."

After a fifteen-minute break, they paddled into the sun. Soon, they found their campsite and set up camp for the last time.

"Tom and I are gonna catch dinner. We're runnin' low on food," said Bob.

Bob and Tom left to fish and Emma retreated to the tent to lay down.

Mark sat on a rock and dangled his feet in the lake. Penny sat beside him and dipped her toes into the cool water.

"Did you get any sleep last night?" Penny asked Mark.

"Yes, but not enough. I think we'll sleep hard tonight."

Penny flicked the water with her foot. "I know I'm young and naive, but can I share something with you?"

"Of course. Go ahead."

"Emma and I met two weeks ago, but we'll be friends forever. You can't endure this trip and not form a lifelong bond. Emma is special to me, and I won't let you hurt her. She tried hard to dismiss her attraction to you and focus on the trip. She didn't come here to fall in love, she came to conquer the Boundary Waters. Think about your words and actions before you go any further. Be careful with her. She's special."

"Penny, don't let anyone tell you you're young and naive. You're wise for such a young woman. You're right. Emma *is* special. I promise to be careful with my words and actions."

Several hours later, Emma held Mark's hand at the campfire with the team after the grilled fish dinner.

"Thanks for the fish dinner, Bob," said Emma.

"Do you realize we've eaten our last dinner in the wilderness? We'll be back at the lodge tomorrow afternoon," said Penny.

Emma clasped her hands together. "The lodge! I can't wait for a bed, a jetted tub, and a fancy meal. I'll never forget this adventure, but I'm ready for comfort."

"I'm with you there, sister," said Penny. "G'night, everyone."

"I need sleep," said Emma. She patted Mark's thigh, but before she stood up, he kissed her on the lips in front of the team. She blushed and touched her lips.

"Goodnight," said Mark.

The hot sun baked in a cloudless sky on the final day of the trip. Mark hurried through the morning chores and practically flew into the canoe. His chest pounded with anticipation for the end of the journey.

The team chatted as they paddled.

"Tell me your favorite part of the trip," Jim said to the group.

"Skinny-dipping," Penny giggled.

"The different animals," said Bob.

"The scenery," said Tom.

"Late-night chats," said Mark.

"New friends," said Emma.

He caught Emma's gaze and they shared a long look until her face broke into a wide smile and her cheeks flushed red.

The team completed their last portage of the trip and entered the final lake. Mark, slower in a canoe by himself, brought up the rear. Emma's ponytail flapped in the breeze, and her tanned arms showed off her sculpted muscles. She talked and joked with Penny as they paddled the final stretch. Emma had stolen his heart, and he longed to hold her again. Alone.

The lodge sat at the end of the expansive lake, and Mark's heart almost beat out of his chest as they neared their final destination. Two hours later, the dirty and hungry group arrived at the dock.

The team unloaded the gear, pulled the canoes onto shore, and assembled in the lodge's conference room. The kitchen staff of the Northern Woods entered the conference room with bottles of champagne for the group to toast their success. Corks flew and the team cheered the completion of the trip. Jim snapped a final picture of the group with champagne glasses raised in a toast to success.

Jim addressed the group. "First, you survived a Northern Woods adventure. Congratulations! This team endured one of the hardest trips I've ever guided. We helped the man with the lost kayak, made it through a record storm, and aided in a medical emergency. I'm impressed! The staff informed me that Helen is in stable condition at a Duluth hospital. She'll stay in the hospital for a few days following a minor surgery this morning. Her children are on their way to her."

The lodge staff passed out room keys, and Mark took a swig of champagne and searched for Emma to celebrate. He twisted and turned in the conference room, but she'd vanished. Where did she go?

"Hey Jim, where did Emma go?"

"She grabbed her key and hit the elevator."

"Thanks."

Mark picked up his key and gear, along with his extra luggage, and popped into the lodge gift shop. He couldn't remember the last time he purchased condoms, but he paid for his purchase and rode the elevator to the third floor. He stood on the threshold of the expansive room with its large bed. He dropped his gear at the foot of the bed and stripped off his dirty clothes. After a shower and a shave, he slipped on clean clothes and rode the elevator down to the second floor.

Chapter Eighteen

A KING-SIZED FOUR-POSTER bed with fluffy pillows and a beautiful quilt welcomed Emma. The afternoon sun streamed in the large picture window and flashed across photographs of the gorgeous Boundary Waters scenery on the walls. She walked into the bathroom and gasped at a walk-in shower; huge, jetted tub; and vanity full of complimentary products. Emma dropped her pack and extra luggage on the ground beside the bed. Her hat found a home on the nightstand. She stripped out of her dirty clothes and turned on the shower. The jacuzzi tempted her, but she wanted to be clean before a soak in the tub.

The hot shower pummeled her back as puddles of dirty water poured down the drain, washing away the enormous physical and emotional toll from the trip. Emma shampooed her hair and shaved her legs. When her fingers turned pruny, she turned off the water and wrapped her body in a fluffy towel. She wandered out to the room, and the familiar view from the picture window in her room conjured images of her adventure in her mind. Once dry, she moisturized, styled her hair, brushed her teeth, and admired her toned body in the mirror. Her arms and shoulders showed the results of hard, physical work. Emma slipped on a pretty pink bra and bikini bottom from her luggage—and then a knock at her door interrupted her.

"Hang on," she called. She threw on the plush robe provided by the lodge and opened the door.

Mark stood on the threshold in shorts and a T-shirt. His clean-shaven face broke into a wide smile, and he smelled like soap. He walked into her room and locked the door behind him.

"Mark?"

Mark stepped toward Emma and placed both of his hands on her face. He pressed his wet lips against hers. Emma tasted minty toothpaste and welcomed his kiss. The tentative kiss became urgent when Mark parted her lips and slipped his tongue inside to tangle with hers. Their kisses intensified until Mark took a breath and kissed her forehead and eyelids. Emma whimpered in his absence and Mark returned to her lips.

Emma grazed her hands down his back and across his tight backside. She pulled him against herself and savored the physical closeness. His large hands stroked her arms and wrapped around her back. The warm robe and the arousal caused her neck and face to flush. Mark bore into her eyes and untied the sash. The robe cascaded to the ground and left Emma in her bra and bikini bottoms. Mark's eyes dilated. "You're beautiful."

Mark pulled his T-shirt over his head and dropped it on top of the robe. He drew his hands over Emma's breasts and stomach to learn the curves of her body. Her pink, satiny bra hid her small globes, but taught nipples pressed through the fabric, and he grazed his thumb across them. Emma panted in response. He kissed her neck and the top of her breasts, but, desperate to feel her skin, Mark lowered one bra strap off her shoulder. Then he removed the other strap and kissed her collarbone. He trailed his kisses to her bare breasts and licked her nipples. Emma's sharp inhales echoed through the room as he explored each one. As soon as he unclasped her bra and let it fall to the floor between them, her breasts tumbled into his large hands. When he sucked a nipple into his mouth and pulled hard, Emma's knees buckled, and he caught her before she fell to the ground. He picked her up with one easy motion and laid her on the bed.

Emma's body throbbed and swelled with each touch from Mark. She lay before him on the bed, clad only in her bikini bottoms. Mark unbuttoned his shorts and let them drop to the ground beside the bed. She licked her lips at his muscular body, and his thick erection strained against his boxer briefs. She opened her arms and welcomed his large body against her small frame, and Mark resumed his attention to her breasts. When he palmed her sex, she whimpered and squirmed for closer contact. She wiggled out of her bikinis and helped him out of his briefs. A collective sigh filled the room when they lay skin to skin. Mark's erection pushed against her thigh, but he dismissed her advances and fingered her slippery center. He groaned at her wetness and explored her folds. Desperate for release, Emma swiveled her hips and yelled, "Ahh!" when he swiped his thumb across her. Her breath quickened when he found his rhythm. It didn't take long until she squeezed her eyes shut and arched her back in a powerful orgasm. She bellowed her release, and her hips bucked on the bed. Emma clamped her thighs together and panted until she came down from her peak.

Her boneless body curved into Mark, and he spread kisses across her face. "You're amazing," said Mark.

Emma pushed Mark to the bed and climbed on top of him. He chuckled as she scrambled onto his body. She rubbed her supple body along his hard planes and kissed his chest. When kisses and touches weren't enough, Mark pulled a condom from his shorts. Once sheathed, he rolled Emma back under him and moved onto her. His midnight-blue eyes sparkled as he entered her, and he exhaled to allow her body time to spread and accommodate his girth. When he seated all the way inside of her, Emma wrapped her legs around him and drew him closer. Their passion rose to a fever pitch as they rocked together. When Mark tipped his head down to suck on a nipple, Emma exploded again. She vibrated in his arms, and he panted through her orgasm. When she regained her wits and urged him to continue, Mark pushed harder and faster and roared his own release. He collapsed into her arms.

"Spectacular sex," whispered Emma.

Mark lifted his head off Emma's shoulder. "What?"

"Spectacular sex. Nicole, my friend in Chicago, always told me everyone deserved spectacular sex." Emma's eyes twinkled. "She's right."

Chapter Nineteen

MARK ROLLED them onto their sides and didn't break their bond. He brushed her hair from her forehead and his fingers trailed the curve of her shoulder. After light kisses and murmurs, Mark said, "Let's try out the jacuzzi."

Mark cleaned up, dimmed the lights, and, when the tub filled with hot water, he helped Emma in and followed behind her. They sank deep in the tub, entangled their legs, and turned on the jets.

"Ahh, my muscles deserve this," said Emma.

"We worked hard."

Mark leaned his head back on the edge of the tub and listened to Emma tell him a hilarious tale of a night locked in a library when she was in college. He followed with the story of when his sister snuck her boyfriend into her bedroom window past curfew. They shared stories until Emma turned around and fit herself in between Mark's legs and he hardened behind her. She caressed his thighs as he played with her breasts and kissed her neck. Water sloshed over the edge of the tub as they entangled.

"Please tell me we have another condom," whispered Emma.

Mark nodded. "We're all set."

They climbed out of the tub and let the bedsheets dry their bodies. The sun set and the room darkened. Mark kissed Emma's hot skin and worked his way down her body. Emma threaded her fingers through his hair but sat up before he reached his destination.

"What's the matter?" asked Mark.

"You don't . . ." said Emma.

"I want to love all of you, Emma."

Emma sank onto the bed and relinquished her body to Mark's ministrations. His lips and tongue laved her folds until she shattered against him. Her body throbbed with ecstasy as she pulled him back up to her. The weight of his body provided a welcome change to her recent celibate life and when Mark entered her a second time, he slowed to a tender rhythm. They murmured to each other as they rocked and moved. He slipped a pillow beneath her hips and hit her deep inside until they climaxed together.

After a brief nap, Mark picked up the phone and ordered room service. A complete steak dinner was delivered, along with a bottle of champagne. They fed each other chocolate cake in bed and talked late into the night. Satiated, Emma snuggled into Mark's arms and slept.

A warm, wet kiss on her lips woke Emma. She opened her eyes to Mark. He stood over her and smiled.

"It's still dark. Why are you dressed?"

"I'm on the early shuttle to visit Helen before I drive home."

His blue eyes pulled her toward him, and she sat up in bed. "Call me?"

"I need your number."

Emma wrote her number on Northern Woods notepaper, and he slipped the paper into his pocket. He wrote his number on the same notepad and left it on the table. Mark kissed her long enough to stir her arousal, cupped her chin and tilted his forehead to hers, and whispered, "We'll talk soon."

The door clicked and Emma sank back into the enormous bed. Her body thrummed with desire and fulfillment. Tender from the sex but ready for another round, she replayed their night. The desire to make love with him again pulled at her soul. She lay in bed until the sun flooded the room and hunger drove her to get dressed and go downstairs.

"Well, well, well. Look at you with swollen lips and a dopey smile. The perfect after-sex glow." Penny winked as she stirred cream into her coffee.

Emma blushed and poured her tea.

Penny patted her arm. "We'll talk later."

After breakfast, they said goodbye to the lodge's staff and loaded into the van. Tom and Bob had left with the first shuttle, so Emma and Penny joined other guests on the later one. Emma twisted her head in the van and peered at the emerald-green forest and sky-blue lake until they disappeared out of sight. She vowed to return.

The group bumped along the dirt road, and the ride smoothed out on the highway. The exhausted guests managed only muted conversation in the van. Penny leaned over to Emma. "So, what happened? You and Mark never showed up for dinner." Penny waggled her eyebrows. "You both missed a fierce game of *Pictionary* in the fireplace room with guests from other trips."

"Mark came to my room after I showered, and we made love and talked long into the night. He left early this morning to visit Helen." She leaned her head against the van window.

"Wow." Penny squeezed Emma's hand. "So now what?"

"I'm not sure." The landscape rushed by outside the window as the question niggled her brain.

Penny and Emma exchanged numbers and hugged goodbye in the Duluth parking lot. "Stay true to yourself. Have a great senior year at college, and keep in touch."

"You're the best. I'm glad we stuck together."

"It's the only way we survived."

"We're an awesome team. You're smart and strong. I want to be like you someday." Penny teared up and pulled Emma into another hug. "You're like my new big sister."

"Aww, you're a sweetie. Drive safely on the way home."

The shuttle's staff unloaded their luggage and Penny drove away. Emma unlocked her car, tossed her luggage in the back, and plugged in her phone. She powered up the GPS and started the journey back to Chicago. Memories of the trip and her sexual night with Mark helped pass the time on the long drive.

She parked her Jeep in front of her nondescript brick building and rested her chin on the steering wheel. Traffic rumbled and sirens blared while foot traffic traveled in front of her building. Her shoulders sagged, and Emma unloaded her luggage. Once settled, she texted Mark.

"Back in Chicago."

Emma waited while the three dots danced on her phone.

Chapter Twenty

MARK PULLED into the hospital's parking garage in Duluth and grabbed a ticket from the machine. He found a spot on the third level, parked, then navigated to the hospital lobby and asked the receptionist for Helen's room number. The sterile hospital smell brought back memories of Meg's illness, but he pushed them away.

Helen was giving a stern look to a nurse and pointing to a TV when he peered into her room. He chuckled and opened the door to the wide-eyed woman. He told the young woman to leave and that he'd help Helen. The nurse scurried from the room.

"I need the TV moved, so the sun doesn't glare on the screen."

Mark walked to the window and lowered the blinds. "They bolt the TV to the wall; it doesn't move. Be careful, Helen, the nurses feed you. You don't want to piss them off."

"Hmph. I'm fine. I've told everyone I'm better and can go home, but they won't listen to me and insist I stay in this prison another day."

"The doctors are in charge. I hear heart surgery recovery is kind of important. Listen to them." He pulled a chair beside her bed and sat down. "Tell me about the plane ride."

Helen rolled her eyes. "Horrible. Just horrible. Flying through the air in a metal tube isn't natural. I like my feet on the ground. Tell me about the rest of the trip."

Mark folded his hands and leaned forward. "After you boarded the seaplane, we waited for Jim to return. Penny scorched some oatmeal before we broke camp and paddled another day and a half. We caught fish for food and Bob and Tom didn't bicker for the rest of the trip."

"It took a medical emergency for them to get along!"

Mark grinned. "You're right."

"And how's Emma?" asked Helen.

Mark's eyes sparkled and his plump lips parted into a huge smile. "Emma and I shared a wonderful night."

Helen patted Mark's hand. "Be careful. Be sure. Remember, she's fragile too."

"I will, Helen, I will. Rest up and I'll call you soon." Mark kissed her on the cheek and returned to his car.

The drive back to Minneapolis proved uneventful. Mark unlocked the front door and walked into his house. As soon as he crossed the threshold, a wall of heavy grief hit him, and he dropped his gear on the floor. He averted his eyes from Meg's smile in the portrait above the mantle in the living room, but her eyes followed him as he walked through his home. Meg's presence filled the space. Photographs graced the tables, and memories of her voice followed him from room to room. A pair of her shoes still lived by the back door, and their wedding album mocked him from the coffee table. Her purse hung on the hook in the foyer, and her scent lingered still on her favorite blanket, draped over the couch. What had he done? How could he have made love to another woman? He ran to the bedroom and slipped on his wedding band. His heart slowed, but his stomach roiled. Guilt smothered him and he collapsed onto the sofa as his phone dinged a text from Emma. He texted her back —"Sleep well"—but deleted the message and typed, "We'll talk soon." His finger paused over the send button and then deleted the message. He typed, "I'm home, too," hit send, tossed his phone onto the table, and wept.

A hamburger with the works and fries satisfied Emma's hunger, and she folded her laundry and went to bed. Sore and exhausted from the trip, she snuggled under the sheets and tried to block the incessant noise of the city to dream of Mark.

She woke up after a solid twelve-hour sleep and pulled her leaden body out of bed to open her blinds. Rain lashed the panes, and gray clouds blanketed the city. Mark had texted her after they returned home, and her fingers itched to call him and hear his deep voice. She skipped her run and stood in a hot shower instead. She slipped on leggings, thick socks, and a sweatshirt and ate a late breakfast. After she read the news online and caught up on her social media accounts, she steeled herself and dialed the phone.

"I'm back in Chicago, Mom."

"We're glad, dear. Did you relax?" asked her mother.

"I canoed and camped the lakes of the Boundary Waters for ten days. I can't wait to tell you about my journey. A bear tried to eat our food and I slept in a tent on the ground. I survived poison ivy and learned how to cook over a campfire."

"Don't fabricate stories, it's childish." Her mom blew out a breath. "I've had a horrendous few weeks. The movers broke three vases. The landscapers haven't mowed the grass, and the bathroom wall color is all wrong. You have no idea. Well, I'm off to the club. Visit soon!" Her mom clicked off the phone.

Emma stared at the phone and shook her head. Nope. Not this time. She dialed her mom again.

"Whatever is the matter, Emma?" asked her mom.

"I want to tell you about my trip, and I think Dad would love to hear about it, too. Put me on speaker."

"I don't have the time—"

"You don't *have* the time, or you don't want to *make* the time?"

Emma's mother exhaled loudly. "What's gotten into you?"

"I survived the Boundary Waters!"

Emma waited for a retort from her mom and, after a minute of silence, Emma said, "Bye, Mom."

She texted her girlfriends in their group chat. "Back in Chicago after an incredible trip!"

Jackie texted back, "Let's get together tonight! Eight o'clock, my place? Bring wine."

Later that afternoon, Emma rode the train back from the grocery store. The Northern Woods ad on the wall triggered memories, and she reminisced about the trip for the rest of the ride. Her phone buzzed in her pocket as she exited the train. She descended the stairs to the street and scurried around the corner to muffle the clacking of the train.

Her shoulders sagged when Mark's name wasn't on the screen. "Hi Dad. I'm glad you called."

"Sweetie, I want to hear all about your trip. Can you talk?"

Emma smiled. "I'm on the street. I'll call you back as soon as I get home."

"Great!"

Emma unloaded her groceries and settled into her loveseat to regale her dad with tales from her trip. Before their long talk ended, her dad said, "I hope you and your mother can repair your relationship."

"Me too. She needs to accept the fact I'm not perfect and never will be. I've never lived up to her expectations, and I'm done trying."

"Understood."

"Dad, I might move out of my apartment. I'm tired of the city."

"I think that's a great idea. I'm so proud of you."

Emma hung up with her dad and checked her phone for a message from Mark. She shrugged at his silence.

Jackie swung open her door and smiled. "Welcome back! You're *tan*. Come on in, the girls are here." Emma carried a bottle of wine and a plate of brownies and she followed Jackie into her home. She hugged her friends in the kitchen.

"I want to hear about your trip," said Alyssa. "Did you see any animals? Did you sleep in a tent for ten days?"

"You had sex," stated Nicole.

Emma's skin flushed under Nicole's assertion, and she grinned. The girls cheered and Emma held up her hand. "I'll tell you all my tales, but I need a glass of wine first." Jackie poured her a glass, and she filled her plate with snacks and a brownie.

They moved into the living room. Emma chose the leather recliner, tucked her legs under her, and sipped her wine.

"I still can't believe I survived ten days in the wilderness. I got chigger bites on my stomach and poison ivy on my butt!" Jackie winced. "The medicine worked, and I didn't need the steroid shot." Emma bit a chip. "A moose ate his lunch near us. They're huge and kinda ugly. I skinny-dipped with the other women, and we almost got caught by the guys. A few nights later, a bear tried to climb a tree to eat our food bag, and there was a terrible storm. My canoe partner and I got lost in the woods. We hauled gear over mud and rocks and beaver dams."

"Yeah, yeah, bears and storms. Who's the mystery man?" asked Nicole.

"Mark's from Minneapolis and a few years older than me. He's kind and helpful and I like him a lot, but it's complicated." Emma sipped her wine. "He's a widower."

Jackie set down her wine glass. "A *widower?*"

"Who cares about that? What does he look like?" asked Alyssa with a smile. She chomped on a pretzel.

"He's tall with broad shoulders and dark hair. He's got silver sideburns and a chiseled jaw. His voice is deep and quiet."

"Dreamy," said Nicole.

Emma nodded and continued. "I'm not gonna divulge *all* the details, but I *will* say I know what Nicole means by 'spectacular sex.'"

"Well done, Emma!" Nicole clinked her glass with hers.

Jackie wrinkled her nose. "Wait. Where is he? Minneapolis is pretty far away. Is he still grieving? When will you see him again? How did you leave things?"

"Mark took my number on the last morning, and then he curled my toes with a goodbye kiss."

Jackie shook her head. "I don't know about this."

"Jackie, give her a break," snapped Nicole.

Emma set down her wine and sat up straight in her chair. "We survived two weeks in the wilderness together and shared a sensual night. This wasn't a fling."

"We don't want to see you hurt again," said Jackie.

Emma bit off a large bite of brownie. "I know. I'll be careful. Now, catch me up on all the Chicago gossip I've missed."

The girls traded gossip and stories, and Emma glanced at

her phone through the night. No messages from Mark. When she arrived home, she texted him. "Would love to talk tonight. Call me?" She went to bed and left her ringer on, but her phone remained silent through the night.

Mark dragged himself around his house the rest of the weekend. He lived in a robe and, by Sunday afternoon, sat amongst empty pizza boxes and beer bottles. The TV droned baseball games on an endless loop. He listened to his coworkers babble on through a myriad of meetings at work on Monday and met Rick for a beer on Tuesday.

"Tell me about the trip," said Rick.

Mark loosened his tie and took a pull of his beer. "We hit some weather about halfway through, but it all worked out okay."

Rick's eyes narrowed. "The weather? Are you crazy? You travel for two weeks through pristine wilderness, and your only comment is about a spot of bad weather? What gives?"

Mark took another pull on his beer and set it on the high-topped table. He picked at the label and blew out a breath. "I met a woman."

Rick slowly nodded. "Ahh . . ."

Mark twisted his wedding band. "An adorable, spunky woman from Chicago came on the trip, and I fell fast and hard. We got together in the lodge, but then I came home—to the house and to Meg." He hung his head. "I betrayed Meg."

Rick leaned forward in his chair. "You didn't betray Meg. She's gone. You're allowed to live your life. How did you leave things with the woman?"

"I told her I would call. She texted me asking me to, but I can't." He twisted his ring around and around. "I don't think I can do this."

"Why don't you talk to Meg about it?"

"Are you serious?"

Rick shrugged. "It might help." He cleared his throat. "Have you . . . sorted Meg's things?"

"I tried to sort through her clothes a few months ago." Mark rested his forearms on the table and whispered, "It's hard."

"Start with something small."

Mark nodded and finished his beer. He threw a twenty on the table. "I need to head home."

The wind blew her ponytail as Emma ran along the lakeshore. She was passing a woman pushing a stroller when her phone rang. The screen blinked Mark's name, and she smiled and answered. "Mark?" said Emma, out of breath. "I'm glad you called!" She stopped and sat on a bench.

"Are you on a run?"

"Yes, but I'm on a bench now. How're you?"

His voice dropped. "Um . . . okay."

Emma knitted her eyebrows together. "What's wrong?"

"Listen, Emma . . . can we talk?"

Noise along the lakeshore muffled and her heart raced. "Of course."

"I'm attracted to you, and I'll never forget our incredible night together." He paused and exhaled. "But—" Mark's voice broke. "But I . . . um . . . can't," he whispered. He coughed and sniffed and then said, "I'm sorry."

Tears welled in Emma's eyes. Grief filled the line, and she wanted to reach through the phone and hold him. "Can we talk about this?"

She heard a sob, and then he said, "Don't wait for me."

"I'll miss you." Emma hung up the phone and brought her knees to her chest and hugged her body as she shook. The sailboats on the lake blurred into a kaleidoscope of color through her tears.

Emma gave up on her run and shuffled home. She curled up on her bed and called Nicole, but her phone went to voicemail. Alyssa didn't answer either. Jackie picked up on the first ring.

"Hey, Emma, what's up?"

"Jackie?" Emma whimpered.

Jackie said, "I'll be over in twenty minutes."

Jackie stood at Emma's door with a pint of chocolate chocolate chip. Emma took the ice cream, and Jackie grabbed two spoons from the silverware drawer and joined her on the bed. They sat cross-legged while the heat and street noise drifted through the open window. "What happened?"

Tears streamed down Emma's face, and Jackie handed her a tissue and put her arm around her friend. "Mark called me this morning. All he said was he couldn't do this and told me not to wait for him." Emma shoved a heaping spoonful of ice cream into her mouth. "You can say, 'I told you so.'"

"Aww, I'm sorry. And I'm sorry for doubting you, but the death of a spouse is tough."

"I know. But we bonded on the trip and shared an incredible night together in the lodge. I miss him. He filled my body and soul, and I want to be with him."

"Love takes time."

Emma sat back on the bed and licked her spoon. "One night, a few months ago, I passed a couple all over each other in the hallway of my apartment building. They couldn't even wait to unlock their apartment door to be together. Mark and I share an electricity I never had with Craig. Even at the start of our relationship, Craig and I always made it through the door."

"Mark may never be ready."

Emma ate another spoonful of ice cream and shook her head. "I'm not ready to give up on him yet."

Chapter Twenty-One

It was July, and the city bustled around Emma. She lay on the beach with her headphones in to while away the days. She daydreamed of Mark and fought the urge to call him every day. Her appetite waned and dark circles formed under her eyes, but she drove out to the suburbs and toured a few apartment complexes. The commute time and generic landscape squashed any further ideas to live in the suburbs and teach in the city.

A few nights later, Emma's girlfriends dragged her to a club. She danced and chatted with the girls, but didn't want to flirt with men and left before midnight. The train clacked above her as she walked the twelve blocks home in the cool breeze off the lake. Two blocks from home, she was crossing a street when someone shoved her into an alley.

"Hey!" Emma shouted.

A guy with a dirty sweatshirt and a ball cap over greasy, dark hair slammed her to the wall, reached into his jeans, and snapped open a knife. Emma's eyes went wide as the man placed his finger on her lips and said, "Shh." He shook his head slowly back and forth as the knife glistened in the streetlamp.

The man snatched her purse from her shoulder, collapsed the knife, and ran around the corner. He hadn't said a word. Emma sank to the ground in a muddy puddle. She wrapped her arms around her legs and shook as she cried.

After a sleepless night, Emma lay in bed as the day dawned and light filtered into her room. A ray of sun found its way through the blinds and landed on her hiking boots by the door. The scuffed and dirty boots took her thoughts back to the trip and how Mark had told her she was strong. She flung the covers off and pulled her laptop from her school bag. She snuggled back in bed and typed in a search for teaching jobs near the Boundary Waters. It couldn't hurt to look, right? Her gritty eyes scrolled through openings, and one caught her attention. It was for a kindergarten through second-grade teacher in a small district with one elementary building. A multigrade classroom intrigued her, and an abundance of curricula ideas flew through her brain. The district was located in a small town on the Lake Superior coast, about a half-hour north of Duluth and two hours east of Northern Woods. The job started after Labor Day. She chewed her bottom lip and opened her resume in another tab.

By late afternoon, she'd emailed her completed application, cover letter, and resume to the superintendent. She went for a run and ordered a pizza for dinner and longed to talk with Mark, but only stared at his name in her phone and left him alone.

Over the next few days, she applied to three jobs in Minnesota and one at a private school in Wisconsin. By the end of the week, she'd participated in a phone interview about the multigrade classroom and received a rejection from the school in Wisconsin. The principal of the school on the Lake

151

Superior coast invited her for an in-person interview, and she booked a flight to Duluth for the last week in July. She pushed aside her sadness and prepped for the interview.

The monstrous lake crashed waves along the rocky shore and the endless evergreens filled every open space on the drive up the coast north of Duluth. The morning interview with the principal went well, and Emma was asked to stay and interview with the superintendent after lunch. The principal took her out to lunch at the local diner, and Emma asked her questions about the area and school as she ate a salad.

"Are there apartment complexes near here?"

"There are apartment complexes in Duluth—thirty miles from here. But the winter weather can ruin a commute. There are quite a few rental houses in town."

"How's the parental involvement in the school?"

"Excellent. We're a small community and residents know highly rated schools help property values. Everyone chips in to support the district."

They chatted through lunch and drove back to the district offices, where she met with the superintendent for an hour in his office. His easy-going manner relaxed her and they discussed curriculum and behavioral management techniques for multigrade classrooms.

Her return flight was uneventful. She picked up dinner on the way home and watched a TV show before bed.

Two days later, her phone rang in her beach bag and her heartbeat kicked up a notch. She rolled over on the sand and fished her phone out of the bag. Was it Mark? The school? She swiped the screen, sat up on her beach towel, and said, "Hey Jackie, how're you?"

Jackie's sobs echoed over the phone and Emma couldn't understand her words. "I'm at the beach. I'll be over in an hour."

She gathered her towel and bag and walked back across the street to her apartment to change clothes. The hot train sped through the city, and she got off at the stop closest to Jackie's house. She pounded on Jackie's door, but no one answered. The doorknob turned and she pushed open the front door to a quiet house. Emma wrinkled her forehead—something was different. At first glance, it appeared normal, but upon closer inspection, some items had vanished. The couch sat against the back wall, but the leather recliner was gone, leaving dimples in the carpet. The end table and lamp were in their rightful place against the side of the couch, but the coffee table and candlesticks were missing. Emma walked through to the kitchen and discovered the chairs shoved in a corner. The table had disappeared. She found Jackie curled up on the bedroom floor where the bed used to be.

"Jackie?" Emma rubbed her distraught friend's back. "Did you get robbed?"

Jackie sat up and blew her nose. Her puffy face and red-rimmed eyes distorted her appearance. "I wish."

"What happened?"

Jackie shoved a piece of crumpled paper into Emma's hands. It was a letter. She read the note and blew out a long breath. "He loves another woman?"

Jackie nodded, her bottom lip trembling.

"But what happened to all the furniture?"

"When we moved in together seven years ago, we split all our costs down the middle—including the furniture we bought for the townhouse. So, while I visited my parents last weekend, he took his half and left me the note. Seven years. I devoted seven years to that jackass and now I have to move." Jackie collapsed back onto the ground in another round of sobs.

Later, Emma encouraged her downstairs and made her a cup of tea and a piece of toast. They talked into the night and before she left, she told Jackie she'd help her look for an affordable apartment. She hugged her friend and caught the train back downtown.

The train sped along the tracks, and Emma pulled her phone from her purse. A missed call notification appeared on her screen. She listened to the message and smiled for the first time in a month.

Chapter Twenty-Two

MARK MOVED through life like a robot in the weeks that followed the trip. He worked and returned home to eat frozen dinners and stare at the flatscreen on the wall, but beer and sports on TV didn't fill the emptiness.

One Saturday morning in July, he lay in bed after a sleepless night. Thoughts of Emma and Meg swirled and tangled in his mind. The sun streamed in through the windows and splashed ribbons of light on the bedroom walls. Meg loved sunny Saturdays.

He dressed in shorts, a polo shirt, and boat shoes. After lunch, he bought a bouquet of lilies at a flower shop and drove to the cemetery, north of the city. He'd visited Meg's grave every week after her death, but visits dwindled in the winter. He'd last visited on the anniversary of her death in April, three months ago. She was buried in a well-maintained cemetery with a parklike setting. Today, the mowed grass smelled like summer. He found her gravestone and wiped grass clippings from the top, laid the lilies on the ground, and sat next to Meg.

"Meg, I went on a canoe trip and met a woman. I tried to

dismiss my attraction to her, but she pulled me like a magnet."
Mark picked at the grass and remembered his first kiss with
Emma by the campfire. Then he remembered how he'd yanked
her ankle out of the mud and laughed out loud. Mark paused.
The breeze blew, and he remembered Meg's final words to him.

*Mark sat beside Meg's bed in the late-morning spring sun
and held her hand. She opened her eyes and smiled. "Mark, I
love you. I've loved you since the moment I laid eyes on you.
Please promise me you'll go on with your life. You are a
wonderful man, and you deserve a family and someone to share
your loving heart." Tears leaked from Mark's eyes as he closed
his hand around hers and bowed his head in sorrow.*

A weight lifted from his shoulders. "Meg, I will always love
you." He kissed her gravestone, promised to visit soon, and
drove home.

Mark wrote a small to-do list on a notepad while he drank his
coffee the morning after his visit with Meg. But he fiddled
around with a broken latch on a cabinet door and pulled a few
weeds in the front yard before he got up the courage to tackle
his list.

First, he slipped the wedding band off his finger and stored
it in a ring box he found in the top drawer of his dresser. Next,
he dusted off the wedding album and boxed and stored it in the
guest-room closet. Five bags filled full of Meg's beautiful
clothes sat by the front door. After lunch, he walked from room
to room and gathered framed photos of Meg. The tissue-
wrapped photos filled two boxes in the closet beside the
wedding album.

. . .

On his way to work Monday morning, he stopped at a donation center. The woman behind the counter opened the bags and gasped. "Oh my, these are beautiful clothes! Our young women who can't afford interview clothes will appreciate these gorgeous items."

"They belonged to my late wife."

She removed her glasses. "I'm sorry for your loss. It's difficult to sort through the personal items of a loved one."

Mark shifted his weight from foot to foot. "Um, do you take coats?"

"Of course. Thank you for your generosity."

Mark sorted and bagged Meg's clothes and the rest of her personal effects over the next few weeks. The one item left on Meg's side of the walk-in closet brought tears to his eyes. Meg had spent days and days with her mom and sisters searching—until she found the perfect princess gown. She'd cried when he helped her remove it on their wedding night. He called his mother-in-law and offered it to her. She sniffled into the phone and thanked him.

The first week in August, Mark returned home from work to find a small package from Northern Woods in his mailbox. After he'd changed out of his suit and tie and grabbed a beer from the fridge, he settled in on his patio and opened the package. The pictures Jim had taken on their trip filled his hands. As he leafed through the stack, he grinned and reminisced about the trip until one image stopped him. He straightened in the chair and lifted the image off the stack, and the rest of the photos scattered on the patio table. The snapshot was of him and Emma on a log beside the campfire. The picture came alive in his hand and the spark between them jumped out of the photo. He held her hand and they gazed at each other. Emma's radiant smile reached her chocolate-brown eyes, amused by a story or a joke. Mark clasped the photo and sucked in a breath at the unmistakable love in his own expression.

The porch chair crashed to the ground when Mark jumped up and slammed into the house. Clothes, toiletries, and camping gear found their way into duffles and then into his Tahoe as he formulated a plan. He hauled his canoe from the garage and was securing the ties on his SUV when his phone rang.

"Hey, what's up?" he asked Rick.

"I've got two tickets to the Twins game tomorrow night. Wanna go?"

"Sorry, buddy. I can't."

"Why not?"

"I'm headed to Chicago."

Chapter Twenty-Three

EARLY THE NEXT MORNING, Mark balanced the picture on his dashboard and plugged Emma's address into his GPS. His foot pressed heavy on the gas as he sped out of Minnesota. Hours later, the highway lanes multiplied as he approached the city of Chicago, and the thick traffic and quick pace of the drivers caused sweat to pour down his back. His GPS didn't recognize the underground roads, and he circled the same area around Lower Wacker five times before he stopped and asked for directions.

The parking spot in front of Emma's building was barely big enough for his Tahoe, but he squeezed it in and grabbed the picture off the dashboard. He pressed the buzzer for Emma's apartment. No answer. After another press of the buzzer, he blew out a breath and leaned against his SUV to wait.

A half hour passed, and he walked around the block. He sidestepped around people and strollers, and he averted bikers. When he rounded the corner by Emma's apartment, a kid on a skateboard swerved and Mark stepped to the left to avoid a collision—but he bumped into someone else.

"Hey!" Emma growled as her bag of groceries spilled onto the sidewalk, and then she yelped when he caught her eye. *"Mark?"*

Mark ran to snatch a head of lettuce and a tomato before they rolled into the street, and Emma loaded taco shells and ground beef back into the bag.

"Mark? What are you doing here?" asked Emma as she stood up with the repacked bag. People flowed around them on the sidewalk.

"I came to see you."

Emma bit her lower lip. "You didn't call."

"I was afraid if I called, you'd tell me not to come. Look at this." He pulled the photo of the two of them out of his pocket.

"A photo from our trip? Mine came in the mail yesterday. What about it?"

"Can we go inside and talk?"

Emma nodded.

They walked up the dingy stairwell and Mark plucked Emma's groceries out of her arms so she could unlock the door.

"You live in a place with four locks on your door?"

"It's fine," she mumbled.

Mark grunted and set her bag down on the tiny kitchen counter. He surveyed her apartment. Boxes littered every available corner. Some were labeled 'clothes,' others 'kitchen dishes,' and a stack near the couch was marked 'school.'

"What's with all the boxes?"

Emma closed her fridge and faced him. "I'm moving."

Moving? His pulse raced. Was he too late? Did she meet someone else? Chicago was already six hundred miles from Minneapolis. Was she moving even farther away?

He cleared his throat and steeled his nerves. "You

mentioned on the trip you wanted to move out of the city. Where're you going?"

"I found a teaching job a half-hour north of Duluth on the Lake Superior coast."

Mark let out a breath and whistled low. "Beautiful area."

"Yeah, it's a multigrade classroom, and I rented a house in town. I move in two weeks." She crossed her arms over her chest. "You didn't answer my question. What are you doing here?"

Mark picked up her hands, and the energy snapped to life between them. "I'm sorry I pushed you away. Getting to know you on the trip was amazing, and our magical night together was the stuff of fairytales. My plan to venture into a long-distance relationship with you blew up in my face when I walked through my front door. The grief overwhelmed me, and I drowned in guilt. I thought my only option was to push you away. But you were always on my mind, and I couldn't let go of you—of us. So I worked through things with Meg and made a lot of progress with my grief. This picture pulled me all the way out of the abyss. The way we look at each other . . . we share something special." He handed Emma the picture and she studied it. "Will you come with me to the Boundary Waters for a week? We'll be alone. I rented a cabin in Misty Lake, and we can hike and canoe and talk. I want to give us a chance. Do you have time to come with me?"

An electrical storm raged across Emma's skin from Mark's touch, and she fought to reign in her libido. Did she have time to spend a week in the Boundary Waters with him? She surveyed her space. Everything was packed except for a few clothes and essential kitchenware. The truck was scheduled, and her mail was already being forwarded to her new address. She'd broken her current lease and resigned from her job. She definitely had the time, but the *real* question remained: should she open her heart up to him again?

She set the picture down on the counter and touched his cheek with her hand. She looked deep into his eyes and said, "I can't believe you're here."

"I can't believe it took me this long to get here."

A tiny crack in Emma's heart emerged, and they talked throughout the afternoon and made tacos for dinner. Later, they snuggled together on her bed as the buildings lit up in the dark night outside Emma's window. Mark talked in low tones about working through the grief and his acceptance of Meg's passing. Emma listened to his words but took her cues about his feelings from his eyes. Finally, as the clock turned over to another day, Emma said, "Kiss me."

They fused together like puzzle pieces, and a rainbow of color beamed behind her eyes as their lips connected. Within seconds, she raised her arms, and he lifted the tank top off her body. She fumbled with his shorts, and he freed her breasts from her bra. She sighed as his large hands cupped her globes and thumbed her nipples. They shucked the rest of their clothes in record time, and she cried out when they joined and didn't care who heard her out the open window.

Emma packed her duffle and they left for Minnesota the next day. They reminisced about their trip and sang along to the radio. Emma talked about her job search and Jackie's breakup. Mark's knuckles turned white on the steering wheel when she regaled him with the story of the mugging, so she changed the subject to a recent movie release. Dusk settled over the SUV as they slowed through Ely. They drove north past the small city and turned down a side road. Mark navigated the final ten miles without the benefit of streetlights. He parked, grabbed their duffle bags, and guided Emma to the cabin in the dark. He used a flashlight to illuminate the lock and opened the door with a code. They dropped their duffles on the floor and found the bedroom. Emma pulled him to her, wrapped her arms around him, and kissed him senseless. They fell to the bed and slept in each other's arms.

Emma woke to Mark's soft snores. She grabbed a fleece blanket from the bottom of the bed and explored the cabin. The bathroom featured all the requisite parts. Emma wandered out to the main room and discovered a worn couch and a scuffed coffee table. The dated kitchenette would suffice for a few days. She walked out the door and found herself on a small porch facing a private lake. She wrapped the blanket tighter around her naked body, and she listened to the loons on the lake and breathed in the clean air. Her heart slowed as she acclimated to the natural landscape.

Mark stepped onto the porch in his boxer briefs and wrapped his arms around her.

Emma leaned her head on his shoulder and sighed. "Good morning."

"Hungry?"

Emma smiled and nodded.

"Let's go into town for breakfast. I'm starving."

Mark and Emma dressed and drove into the town of Misty Lake and parked in the square. They held hands and walked down the sidewalk to the local diner.

"Isn't this the adorable town closest to Northern Woods?" asked Emma. "I remember the one blinking stoplight."

"Yep."

A small cafe elicited sweet smells and tourists flooded the corner market. The gazebo in the town square sheltered a few women who sipped coffee and chatted. Two boys played catch nearby.

"You wouldn't need four locks on your door here."

Emma giggled. "Nope."

Bells over the diner door jingled their arrival, and they waited for a table in the noisy restaurant. Once seated, Emma sipped her tea and Mark blew on his coffee.

"Tell me about your new job."

Emma's inner cheerleader jumped for joy whenever he asked about her life. "It's in a tiny school district and my classroom will include three grades of kids. I'm excited for the curriculum challenges and the social opportunities for the kids." He nodded, so she went on to describe her theme for the year and other ideas she had for the unique classroom.

"And you rented a house?"

"Yep. It's a few miles from the school and on a quiet street. It's a bungalow, but I don't need much. I can't wait to live in more than one room, though."

"We should check out your new town while we're here."

Emma blinked in surprise. "It's a few hours away—on the coast."

Mark held her hands over the table. "It's important to you and it'll be fun."

The fissure in Emma's heart widened. Their server delivered Emma's blueberry pancakes and Mark's omelet. Emma poured syrup over her plate, and Mark said, "It's pretty cold up here in the winter."

"I mastered the Boundary Waters. I'll survive." Emma winked and ate a forkful of pancakes.

They spent the afternoon in Mark's canoe on the private lake. When they reached the middle of the lake, Mark set down his paddle. He scooted up to the middle of the canoe and beckoned to Emma. She met him in the middle, and they kissed as the canoe rocked them side to side. Once back on shore, they changed into swimsuits and returned to the lake. Mark led Emma to a cove and held her in his arms while she wrapped her legs around his torso and her arms around his neck.

They bobbed in the warm water and talked and kissed. Mark dropped the straps of her suit and kissed her collarbone. She pulled away from him, shimmied out of the suit, and tossed it on the shore. Mark slipped off his suit and enveloped Emma in his arms.

The next afternoon, Emma plugged the location of her new town into Mark's GPS, and they drove two hours to explore the Lake Superior coast. They found her rental house and the school, and then they wandered the streets of the small downtown. As they sat sipping a cocktail before dinner in a restaurant on the lakeshore, Emma confessed her difficult relationship with her mother. Mark didn't offer advice but listened to her frustrations in silent support. During dessert, Mark detailed the drama of four sisters and how his passion for hockey in high school earned him a full ride to the University of Minnesota to play on their team.

Like most nights in the cabin, they talked and made love until the wee hours of the morning, and the rift in her heart grew with each passing day.

On Thursday afternoon, they laced their hiking boots and found a trail into the forest. Emma held Mark's hand around downed trees and muddy puddles until they approached a clearing with a large, flat rock. Mark sat on the rock and pulled

Emma onto his lap. The serious look on his face gave her pause, but his dark-blue eyes sparkled, and she tingled from head to toe when he placed his large hand on her cheek.

"I'm falling in love with you, Emma."

Her heart split wide open to engulf him. "I'm in love with you, Mark." They kissed and pressed into each other, desperate to merge their souls. Mark moved his hands along Emma's curves while she weaved her hands through his hair and shifted on his lap to capture his hardness between her legs. Behaving like fevered teenagers, they struggled back to the cabin and stripped their shorts off on the porch. Mark held Emma against the open door and lifted her onto him. Their moans echoed through the cabin when they joined, and after Mark orchestrated their climaxes together, they collapsed onto the floor.

Emma murmured, "We didn't even make it through the door."

Several hours later, they cooked a frozen pizza and went outside at dusk to build a fire in the firepit.

"Minneapolis is three hours away from your new job, but a lot closer than Chicago," said Mark.

Emma poked a stick in the fire and let the hot flame warm her cheeks. "A teacher's work is compressed during the school year. I plan and grade every night and on the weekends. And I'll spend extra time developing the curriculum for my new class, but I'll have long holiday breaks."

"Tax season is my busy time—December to April. It's crazy busy and I spend eighty hours a week in a suit and tie." Mark's voice dropped lower than his usual baritone and he said, "Can I tell you a secret?"

Emma poked the fire again, and he shoved his hands into his pockets. "Of course."

"I hate being a CPA. There are so many rules, and my office is stuffy and the endless spreadsheets are awful."

Emma furrowed her brow but waited for Mark to continue. An owl hooted and she swatted away a mosquito.

"You know what I've been thinking about lately?" asked Mark.

"No, what?"

"Buying an outfitter store somewhere in the Boundary Waters. I could be my own boss and help people prepare for safe trips into the wilderness."

"Wow! That's a cool idea. Do you know anything about the outfitter business?"

He kicked a stone. "Not really."

Emma snuggled into his shoulder and said, "I bet you could learn."

Emma woke with a start in the middle of the night. The clock read 4:45 a.m., and she touched Mark's side of the bed. The cold sheets sent a shiver up her spine. Her heart rate picked up and her stomach flip-flopped as she slipped Mark's T-shirt over her naked body to investigate. The bathroom and the main living area stood quiet and empty, so she opened the squeaky cabin door and stepped onto the porch. The gray of dawn seeped into the landscape, and she spied Mark's SUV in the drive. She padded off the porch and picked her way down to the lake in her bare feet. Mark, in shorts, sat on the small beach.

"Mark?"

He turned around and smiled. "I didn't mean to wake you."

"It's okay. Are you all right?"

"Yep."

Emma sat beside him as the sun rose over the evergreens in the distance to burn off the thick layer of fog on the lake. She slipped her hand into his. They threaded their fingers together and Mark squeezed her hand and kissed the side of her head.

"I'm gonna do it," said Mark.

"Do what?"

"Buy an outfitter store in the Boundary Waters."

Emma faced him with wide eyes and a smile.

"I figure if you can be brave, so can I."

"Listen," said Emma. They paused and a beautiful loon call echoed over the lake.

"The loons are calling us home," said Emma as she kissed Mark on the lakeshore at sunrise.

Acknowledgments

Thank you to Erin Helmrich and her amazing staff at the Fifth Avenue Press. A special thanks to Casey Gamble and Amy Sumerton for their editing expertise. Their time and patience with this project has been invaluable. Thank you to Kate for reading my very rough first draft. A special thanks to Jen for always reading and critiquing whatever I throw her way! Thank you to Ben and Jane and the rest of my family and friends for their unwavering support. Finally, thank you to Dan —my ultimate cheerleader and partner in everything.

About the Author

Amy Hepp grew up in several locations along the Great Lakes. She is a graduate of Purdue University and settled in a suburb of Detroit with the love of her life. Amy devoured the contemporary romance genre as a sleep deprived young mother of three, needing an escape from reality. All three children are grown, but she's still a pushover for a good love story and is excited to share her love of the Boundary Waters with her readers. Amy is a runner, loves puzzles, and writes from her home in Ann Arbor, Michigan.

CPSIA information can be obtained
at www.ICGtesting.com
Printed in the USA
BVHW052339020922
645879BV00003B/11